T0196192

OUTTA Sbzzz Mind

OUTTA Sbzzz Mind

Sb Waitt

authorHOUSE®

AuthorHouse™
1663 Liberty Drive
Bloomington, IN 47403
www.authorhouse.com
Phone: 1 (800) 839-8640

Published by AuthorHouse   04/25/2012

ISBN: 978-1-4685-5098-6 (sc)
ISBN: 978-1-4685-5099-3 (e)

Library of Congress Control Number: 2012903137

Print information available on the last page.

SOME "N" PORANT STUFF TO
I WANT YOU TO KNOW

Fundamentals: The fundamental within this book is that I like to have fun with my mental abilities. Perhaps you may even say I'm a nut job! Remember I prefer cashews and pistachios the best. Although a hot fudge sundae topped with salted Spanish peanuts is a good combination to me, preferable with the skins on.

Elements: Some of the elements in this book. Well there is a lot of carbon, hydrogen, oxygen, and zinc. For all of you that go on to become scientist in the near future. I'd enjoy a letter sent to me with a list of any elements that I forgot to mention from my brief research into this area; also, send gold, cause that is a great element! I believe you like gold, I do . . .

Disclaimer: I am a professor of Sbologies so that which is read in my book is for your pleasure, entertainment and enjoyment as well as mine. There are truths and facts with the contents of this book, course you'll have to prove them for me; well, choice is better than having to do.

Guarantees: I have no guarantee if you read this book that you will find the meaning of life, solve the problems in the world that we live in or any future worlds that we discover, or attempt to lay claim too there of henceforth quote and unquote.

"Let it be known!" I have not physically hurt any animals or humans in the writing and drawing of this book. I didn't personally kill any of the trees used in making the paper in this book. I have been known to eat my words from time to time so I will do so with a nice burger and fries, along with a chocolate shake to wash it all down with.

Rules: Who says? I like to break rules not laws. Specially the dumb rules that some people place upon themselves; so, I like: eating desert before supper, wearing sneakers at a formal diner, going out and have fun regardless of the dishes being washed or the lawn being mowed, and so what if the laundry isn't folded right away after the drier stops. I like to respect people and not hurt or harm them. I don't have to live other people's lives or belief system as long as we care about one another. A good rule to follow is to live and not 'just' exist.

Beliefs: I believe we originate from the stars so we are all stardust. Thus, we are all here to brighten up one another's lives. May we all bring light into to the world as the stars not darkness. Where shadows fall and are cast may we all be beacons to light the path for those that are lost. We are here to be supportive of one another, to build up not tear down, destroy, or humiliate. My soap box is not tall so that I stand out and be placed upon a pillar, only high enough to be heard and blend in. If you lead with conviction and sound judgment I will follow, if you fall I will pick you up, and if you are injured I will carry you until the proper help comes. Yes I have the ability to lead and will lead; my favorite position and roll is to play second to support the leader and call out to gather his or her flock. I believe we can all make a difference in this world in some way; so, why not!

Making a difference comes in all ways, shapes, and sizes. Think outside of the sandbox and do it. If your insides and instincts tell you an idea you have will make a difference, than it will! I truly believe the harder someone laughs at your ideas is because they are a good idea.

And remember . . . Look for the good and you'll find it, look for the bad and you'll find that too; but, if you look really hard you may see and find aliens.

PEOPLE I WANT TO THANK

And I know there are many more

- My mother and father, I'm sure they had a great Christmas or New Year's Eve party before I was born.
- My Sister Cheryl, she was involved in my art and personal development over the early years. You took me to the first cartoon movie I ever watched at a local movie theatre and put up with all my antics as a child.
- My brother Jim, to who would draw a train on the spot upon request and later helped me go through very difficult times
- Captain Bob, my favorite TV show before school which involved drawing.
- Hank Ketchum, I've enjoyed your cartoons and comic books ever since I could first read.
- To the crew of the Jupiter II, you helped me maintain my sanity during my insanity, insecurity, and being afraid of life and people over the years.
- To all my art teachers, there were several art teachers that I don't remember their name, you kept me interested even when I wasn't; water coloring with a floppy paint brush from school was my least favorite form of art.
- Mr. Allen from Junior High School, I believe you are why I was selected into drafting at Trade School.
- Mr. Bachelor, (vocational drafting teacher 10th through 12th grade) you believed in me and my abilities and realized my potentials.
- Mrs. Southworth I believe was her name during 12th grade art classes. She was a great art teacher! On trash day she'd drag lots of great thrown out junk for us to draw and turn into art. Oh yea, she let me stay in class for a full year even though it was only a half year class.
- Red Skelton, You taught me it was OK to express one's self even though I was a boy, young man, and an adult.
- Dave W., you introduced me to Cat Stevens music at the end on my senior year of school. I've been listening to his songs of life and quest for meaning ever since
- Terry s. From my first ship, you are why I go by Sb today. Where are you today?
- Terry A. and Chief L. You introduced me to CREADO and encouraged me to participate.
- My buddy Howard, you always said to me, "Why do you want to do everything that doesn't come natural to you! Draw!"
- Gary Larson, I enjoy all your cartoons and humor.
- Lyn R., you introduced me to Canon Training and Development
- Donna E., you believed I was an artist before I declared myself one.
- Fran C. your personal growth seminars are the best. You are a part of why I am today.
- Frank G, you kept encouraging me to create a book with my art in it.
- Kat, you got me through the book, Artist Way. Fun memorable times.
- Cindy, my love, my wife, my friend, my all . . .
- My loving children Andrew and Samantha who without I would never have been called dad.

LITTLE BIT OF HISTORY
ABOUT ME

I WAS NOT FOUND ON the door step or crawled out from a rock; I was born into this world as a product of my mother and father in a town called Beverly Massachusetts in the year of 1955 in the month of September. It's a small town about 20 miles north of Boston. The town next door which you may be more familiar with is named Salem. That's where they use to burn and torment people accused of being a witch and today, it's a great place to participate in Halloween fun. Beverly is known as the Birthplace of the US Navy and also so is the town named Marblehead Massachusetts.

You see this ship called the Hannah was built in Marblehead back before we (America) were a recognized country called The United States of America. During the Revolutionary war General George Washington Commissioned the Schooner as our first naval vessel on September 3, 1775. So there has been controversy between Marblehead and Beverly for years and years about who is the real birth place of the US Navy . . . I say, the navy was conceived in Marblehead (where the ship was built) and born in Beverly (when the commissioning of our first US Navy ship took place at Glovers Wharf.) May the USS Hannah sail on forever . . . There is a found plaque stating otherwise, however . . . It doesn't make sense to me. Either does the Navy's birthday being celebrated on October 13th . . . However, the powers that be are the powers to declare whether the 'facts' are not and make up the rest . . . I'm a rebel.

You didn't realize you where going to have a history lesson from this book did ya. Please pay attention now, cause I may include a test at the end of this book. Some added Nfermationn, cause I know you wanna know is; the first person to be a commissioned commanding offer was Nicolson Broughton. He and his crew even captured the British sloop Unity. I like the word sloop and I believe this is the type of ship our modern navy could use today to spruce it up.

Now back to the Who Am I, what I am, where I did it, when and the why stuff . . . I have two . . . err wait a minute . . . What about how . . . Is how supposed to be in there somewhere, is it who, what, when, where, why, and how???? Anyway, I have two older brothers and two older sisters as well. I was fortunate enough to live in the same house my entire youth before joining the navy. I lived close to the ocean; I have always enjoyed the aroma of the salt water of an ocean. When my friends and I walked to the beach it would only take about ten minutes unless we detoured through the cemetery.

I went through the Beverly Public School system for thirteen years. I never went to kindergarten. In forth grade I stayed around an extra year so I could help out the teacher. That's the year when I figured out that the bare minimum grade for me and my mom and dad was going to be a C to pass and keep TV privileges going; I had my priorities . . . My favorite subjects in grade school were drawing, recess, lunch and going home. I excelled in going home! Oh, I almost forgot and an occasional field trip is a worthwhile subject as well . . .

My least favorite subject was spelling . . . Once I received an "A" for that subject one quarter during the 6th grade. So I walks up to the teacher's desk and said, "I believe you made a mistake on my report card?" She answered, "Oh really?" "Yea, you gave me an "A" in spelling?" She looks down to the side draws of her desk and pulls out a folder, turns a few pages, and said, "No! No mistake, you earned and 'A'!" I opened my mouth and nothing came out for a moment or two then I asked, "What, how'd that happen?" She smiles and said, "I only gave one spelling test this past quarter and you received an 'A'." All I could think about is how am I going to explain that grade to my parents?

In Junior High School my goal was to be invisible best I could. I was afraid of the world in school and junior high was the most frightening school years for me. I enjoyed art class, I wanted to drop my lunch class, and I excelled more and more in going home, really fast! These middle schools years, where the years, that the refrigerator became one of my best friends, once I arrived home from school. I believe just about every morning I was too sick to go to school and my mom made be go anyway!

During 9th grade, I was called into my guidance counselors' office when it was time to select my itinerary for high school. I don't ever remember going into his office except for this one time during my stay at Junior High; so why he was called my counselor to this day, I don't have a clue! I was asked by 'my counselor,' "What do you want to do for high school?" I knew dropping grades 10 through 12 was not an option' so I replied, "Not Trade School, Not Business Course, I want College Course." He looks through a folder in front of him, looks up, and asks, "What language do you want to take?" I said, "English." "No, no what foreign language do you want to take?" I answered, "None!" Then he said, "If you don't take an alternate language you're not taking the college course!" I then ask, "Why do I have to take a foreign language," while shaking my head? He then said, "Without a language your choices are Business or Trade school." I didn't understand why the language was so important at that time and or even now to certain degree . . . (When the time comes in life you, me, we . . . will take a language.) Finally I said, "Not Business!" He showed me a list of courses in Trade School and I selected Draftsmen. He then said, "Pick another choice only two from this school will be accepted and go into that class!" I said, "I don't have a second choice . . . I want the Draftsman class and it's that or nothing!" 'Nothing,' most likely meant 'business course at the high school or some other course that didn't interest me in trade school.'

Over the summer, between 9th and 10th grade, it dawned on me what I did. I was amazed afterwards about my decision to elect Trade School in three ways: One, the way I spoke to the guidance counselor was not the way I usually talked in school. I always cowered and gave in especially to authority. Two, I spoke up for myself. And three, that's where all the tough guys go, what was I thinking!!!

For my High School years I went to vocational school (Trade School) to become a Mechanical Draftsman. The High School and Trade School was all connected. We (trade schoolers) were called animals by those in High School . . . I don't remember if we had a name for all those that attended the High School? I had my doubts and I wasn't sure what I got myself into. My doubts weren't about the subject matter it was being in an all boy school. You see, I was afraid of a lot of those guys that made it into trade school and I thought it was going to be a continuation of Junior High. Thankfully, I was wrong and it turned out that my Vocational years of school were my best years of school. I soon became healed of my illness that occurred every morning upon waking up. So, I wanted to go to school for the first time since the second day of First grade. I still excelled in going home, that wasn't always my favorite part of the day, didn't know who was behind me. They all turned out to be pretty good guys after all . . . Not that I set the standards for being pretty good or who am I the one to say who is good and who is not! We are all deserving of respect in life.

After graduating from Vocational school in 1974 I worked as a draftsman in a company called Clintex in Danvers Massachusetts. We designed medical equipment to probe, examine, mend and photograph the eye. Some of my favorite memories were: driving to work with David W. when he'd play his tunes (we'd listen to Cat Stevens music mostly), doodling cartoons at lunch, and I enjoyed working and being with everyone that worked there. George the electronic technician and Mike the shipper introduced me to the world of the Marx's Brothers, W.C. Fields, and some of the other great old comedians. Steve H. introduced me to the humor of Monty Python which was on the PBS network where I soon discovered Doctor Who. Tony R was a singer in the evening, I believe this is why I enjoy going out to coffee house to watch and listen to people performing on stage. Yep, there were a lot of good times and memories. Clinitex was a small company and was a wonderful experience before joining the navy in May of 1976. I remember on April fool's day I didn't go into work or call in sick. I went to the navy recruiters' office to take an entrance exam. Later, I walked into work after 2pm; almost everyone in the company asked me, "Where have you been?" I replied, "I joined the Navy!" They all thought I was telling a good April fool's joke.

I attended Navy boot camp at Great Lakes Illinois from there I flew to San Diego California where I completed basic Sonar training. I was assigned to my first ship at 32nd Street Naval Station San Diego. I will talk more about the navy, my ships and experiences from time to time in my writings next to my art work as well as other times and experiences of my life.

About a year and one half latter after joining the navy is when I started to go by my first initials . . . Sb. I didn't realize at the time, I was in the process of reinventing myself just from this new way of calling out my name. The "Sb" name began when I was on my first ship USS Gray 1054 and we were heading out for an overseas deployment for 6 months. Terry S. wrote everyone's name on the grease board for underway sonar watch stations by first two initials and last names. He then said, "Lets call everyone by their initials only." I believe inside of a week we were back at calling everyone by their first name except me. I liked being called Sb. So to this day 99.9% of everyone I know calls me by some version of Sb . . .

Now since leaving the Navy I still go by the name, "Sb." So, when people ask, "what is your name?" I say, "Sb!" Then they'll say, "No! What is your first name!" and again I'll reply, "Sb." They'll look at me funny and then say, "No, no what are you called by?" I'll answer a little louder, "Sb." "No, what is your first name?" I'll say, "Sb." They'll look at me all confused, shake their head, and stare in my eyes. They'll pause as a light comes on in their mind and ask, "What does Sb stand for?" I'll say, "Sb." What did your parents call you growing up?" I'll smile and answer, "I don't answer to my name that I grew up with anymore." This will go on for some time. Unusually the last thing I say is, "Sb can stand for: Social Butterfly, Stanislavski Balintnikoff, Santa Barbra, or what ever variation of Sb you can come up with." They'll say, OK, Sb." Most times after they accept "Sb" as my name and some people will then ask, "are you ever called an S-O-B? I smile and say, "Yes from time to time I have been called that!" I'm sure as I reflect back over the years; there have been many times when SOB was more appropriate. A few of my friends pronounce the two letters in "Sb." It sounds like, "Sbaah," when the letters are pronounced phonetically. I do like, 'Social Butterfly.'

Some fun stuff I did while in the navy while ashore on liberty . . . Scuba diving, snow skiing (my favorite was in Spain on the Sierra Nevada Mountains), parachuting, lots and lots of restaurants, movies, and exploring foreign ports, driving across America, etc . . . Two of the dumbest things I ever did for fun was . . .

Once I was at this bull fight training camp in Spain. It was enjoyable because no bulls where hurt, no blood, and there was music and humor intermixed; this where I heard the 'Chicken Dance' music for the first time. Near the end of the live show, some of the workers walked into the stands talking with the audience while carrying a bunch of papers. It was a permission slip invitation for anyone to come out into the arena. I signed a waver that was written in Spanish that I didn't understand a single word too or thing about . . . And the next thing you know, I'm in the bull rink . . . We could see eye to eye with the bulls. Thankfully the horns were not sharpened. I did good with the flapping of the cape! (Yes, I said 'good' not 'well!' Ya can turn me into the Grammar Police or one of my past English Teachers if you want too.) When the bull charged me, I'd step aside and he'd run under the out reached cape. I didn't do so 'good' with the two wooden sticks. They were for touching the back of the bull above the front shoulder as the bull charged towards me. The wooden dowels simulated a sword . . . The bull won on that attempt. He got me in the ribs and received a non-simulated bruise. I was sore for a month. Today, I wonder if I'll receive a knock on my door and find out what I really signed in that Spanish document. Perhaps it was an authorization for a retired Toreador to take my home once I he reaches the golden age of 55?

The second dumbest thing I did was in Morocco. About 5 of us were walking around streets and alleys and we came across this snake charmer. He said something to us which none of us understood. He made a motion to me. I thought he wanted me to make an attempt at grabbing the cobra? Well I didn't catch the Cobra, as I gave it two quick passes of my hand around at the snake. I didn't get bit and the snake charmed yelled something at me! He continued mumbling and raging as he pushes the lid down on the basket that housed the snake and he left in a huff . . . I figured the mouth was sewn or the fangs where removed . . . Hmmm, was this a good move on my part? Probable not, it was a good story to tell back at the ship. Maybe learning another language would have been a good idea after all.

I retired from the navy January 1995 at FLTASWTRACENPAC San Diego California (ASW base: Anti Submarine Warfare.) I have two children Andrew and Samantha. I currently live in San Diego California. My children grew up and live not too far from me.

I participate in a charity called Big Animals for Little Kids. I'll write a little bit more about this wonderful organization from time to time and for my last picture in this book. Please look it up on the internet: biganimalforlittle.com I am donating 10% of my earning from this book to the organization. I'm putting ideas together for a coloring book for this group as well and they will receive the majority of the earnings.

I enjoy listening to music of all kinds. I thought when I grew up my taste in music would be set in stone and I wouldn't branch out and listen to any of the new music. I guess I haven't grown up yet. I really like the music I can close my eyes and search my soul, seek the meaning of existence, life, why are we here, and how can I better myself. I find enjoyment in listening to children's music. There are a lot of answers to adult life inside these songs most have determined to be to kid-like to listen too.

I've kind of stopped watching the slasher-horror movies for the most part. There is a couple I still watch however I don't seek new blood for these kinds of movies. I still enjoy the oldies such as: The Marx's Brothers, WC Fields, and Abbot and Costello. I enjoy comedies, action adventures, Science fiction and an occasional chick flick . . . I find I don't have the need to bring children with me when I go to a children's animated movie. Bringing a child or two does make it more enjoyable. Specially one of my Grandchildren

So there is a little bit about me . . . for now!

THIS BOOK IS ABOUT

One hundred pages and then some or so long . . .

THIS BOOK IS ABOUT ME, my humor, outlooks, thoughts, believing in myself regardless of the subject matter, and a reflection of myself. Some times it's simple, sometimes it's twisted, strange, weird, and sometimes it's a little bizarre, irreverent, and sardonic. There is some personal growth information I learned over the years mixed in with a few short stories from time to time. There are some ideas on how I believe, "We can change the world and make a difference."

When I draw, it may start from a doodle or a mark where I place my pencil or pen tip on to the paper. I never know what thoughts will surface out of my mind as they leak upon a piece of paper out of: boredom, excitement, depression, happiness, anger, fear, being clueless, doubt or in disbelief of what I watched, happiness, or some other emotional or reason. The key for me with drawing is to mix it up the drawing and enjoy myself; I'm not as interested in drawing a comic strip with one main character even though some of my friends tell me that's what I 'should' be doing. I'm not in too 'shoulding on myself' these days. Drawing or doing anything is always better when I enjoy myself, what a concept. Oh yea, music is a motivator for me as well; the kind that makes my mind think and wander, touches my soul, generates tears, and sounds good.

While during my navy years from 1976 to 1995 I did my best to hold on to my sketches, ideas, doodles, and scribble the best I could. There was a part of me that said, "Maybe someday . . ." I believe someday is here now. Someday for the most part never comes. It's that built in escape for the days when I don't believe that I'm good enough.

I invented a someday. I call it Sumday! It's when it's both Sunday and Monday, due to the time zones around the world, is happening at the same time. The days overlap so, the day that it is Sunday and Monday I call it Sumday. This gives us all a belief and realization that someday can and will come . . . So the next time Sumday comes around . . . That's a good time to start working on your list of someday wanna do sometime things, ideas, or adventures. It's never too late to start! When you get older it may be called your, "Bucket List."

This idea of Sumday came to me after doing a personal growth seminar about two years ago. The first time I heard Paige talk about "someday" was at least 10 years ago. She would say, "Someday is the eighth day of the week, because it never comes." For years I though about someday and how could I make someday a reality. Well I did as noted in the previous paragraph.

I attended my first personal growth seminars back in 1992 while in the Navy called: CREADO. It started something inside, kind of a way of looking at life and self different . . . At that time I didn't totally believe change in me would happen. Once out of the navy I attended another seminar similar and different to CREADO; this time I participated with more enthusiasm in the personal growth seminar during the early months of 1995! It goes by the name of Cannon Training and Development. So, come on out to San Diego and give experience it Sumday.

With time I may see something new in a particular drawing or doodle that I didn't see before. On a personal level, interpretation is a wonderful thing, it's never right or wrong it's what we/I see or perceive. I own it so whatever you or I think is great and wonderful. Be careful, once our perceptions leave the mouth in the form of words and action, "right and wrong" just might matter then. So these cartoons, drawings, pictures, or what ever you want to call my art work, may you enjoy those you do. Possibly the ones you don't care for will in time grow on you from an experience. And the ones you hate, well that's now. How bout now, or now, or now . . .

I can still remember some of my drawing during my youth, teens, and childhood. Some images never disappear. One time in particular I was drawing a few doodles in my science class in 7th grade. Oh yea Mr. Palonzii's class it was. I sat in the back of the class and usually was very quiet. I was drawing astronauts on the moon, the Command and Service Module linked up to the Lunar Excursion Module around the moon, and a picture of the science teacher with his grin. I even got the part in his hair correct.

He quietly comes over to my desk. I was engrossed in my pencil sketch so I did notice him till the last few moments before he reached his hand out for the pictures. I was caught so I shuffled one drawing in particular to the back of the pile. "What's this?" he asks. I reply, "Just some doodles." He takes them and starts to walk up to the front of the class. The last one in the pile is the one I don't want him to see. Like that's not gonna happen? And then the pause . . . In a low raspy voice increasing in volume to a high raspy sounding voice he blurts out, "Ohhhh, is this a picture of me?" This is where I begin the lies, "No! It's just a doodle." He looks at me and says, "No, it's a picture of me!" He looks right at me and stares me into another lie, "No, no I was doodling. I never know what's gonna end up on the paper when I doodle." He looks at the picture and bobs his head up and down and said, "This is my face." He's shaking his head up and down and he's wearing the same grin I drew in the cartoon character. As he hold the picture out straight and says' "That's the way I part my hair!" He grins and shuffles the side step a few times over tone of my class mates in the front and asks, "Doesn't this look like me? The first student replies, "No!" He moves to another student and asks the same question "Doesn't this look like me?" He receives the same reply. I was amazed when everyone said no! I knew better. He then makes "the" comment, "Perhaps if you paid attention in class more than you drawing . . . blaa, blaa, blaaaaa bla bla!" It's always, "Blaa, blaa, blaaaa, bla bla!" How many times have I heard that before? "Blaa bla this and blaa bla that." It wasn't the last time I drew in his class. I believe he enjoyed putting students at an uneasy position. Now that I look back on that memory, if I was the teacher I would of did the same thing. Milk it for a laugh, enjoy the character drawing, and go back to teaching the subject matter. I don't remember what he was lecturing about at the time? That never mattered. I drew whether I was interested or not! I do wonder if he held on to those drawings or threw them out. The way my mind is thinking goes . . . He held on to doodles and placed them into a scrapbook which he has treasured over the years.

Don't get me wrong . . . Education is very important. If you're not sure about what to take for college classes, sign up for something that sounds fun and appealing to you along with those required courses. Maybe with time those fun classes will help you make a decision. When you're finally done with college and have your degree . . . Continue with the fun classes somewhere.

So this book has a bunch of "N" fermation in it. What's the value of my Nfermation? You'll decide after reading it. It may be useful to you somehow, not sure how? Yet, I have a feeling it will. So enjoy it and use it wisely, specially if you're a wise person. Wise people have a way of using Nfermation wisely. Do I? Will you think I'm a wise and a seasoned person when you reach the end of this manuscript with pictures? The word "manuscript" sounds to me a little more intelligent than the word" book," Do you not agree? Course, I'm a guy growing in age so I'm starting to forget stuff and mix things around from time to time. I've been told by instructors in college that they believe I'm mildly dyslexic, eccentric, off my rocker, bizarre and a good student all in the same breath? OK, So I babble a little too. That can be a good thing. People like to camp out by babbling streams cause it's relaxing and is helpful when the time comes for the time to sleep. Are ya sleepy yet? I do enjoy camping specially on moonless nights away from the city when you can see billions of stars and are able to make out where the Milky Way lies. Whoops this part might belong in the section called, "Little bit of history about me."

Again let me remind you I don't play by the rules for grammar, so if the 'grammar police' is out there please mail my ticket to 11715 Lake Grove Court San Diego California 92131 . . . Spelling was never my favorite subject! Too many rules and exceptions to the rules, I believe. The last book of rules I read was called, "The book of rules," have you ever read it? Oey! Maybe it was call, 'Rules?'" is it important?

What else is in this book? Hmmm, well . . . I suppose if I quit writing you'll start looking at the pictures. Maybe you're the kind of person to jump forward and backwards while looking over the book. That's OK too . . . Ok I'll stop now . . .

CONTENTS

WHO IS THAT PERSON
IN THE MIRROR?

DO YOU EVER LOOK IN the mirror and wonder or say, "Who is that man/woman in the mirror?" I sure do. What have I become? Who could I have been if only . . . ? Sometimes I want to scream. Sometimes I forget the things I use to do for myself and others. The song by Johnny Cash comes to mind, "The Hurt," also Michael Jackson's song, "Man in the Mirror"

How do others perceive me, especially when I doubt myself? Change can come from with in when I come to a realization that I am worthy, valuable and loved. Change also comes from outside sources when inspired, doubt is created, or when provoked.

I don't like change for the most part even though it can and is a good thing. Reinvented self brings forth new ideas, possibilities, and outlooks. I like to draw yet it took along time before I ever called myself and artist. The first time I ever really believed I am an artist was after walking through a Contemporary Museum. This was during a field trip while attended an art class at Miramar College around the 1997 time frame. The exhibits I saw provoked me. I was angry! I came out of there saying if they are artist based on what they created, who or what am I . . . I walked towards my car fuming. Before I got to my car I yelled out loud, "I AM AN ARTIST!" I am trembling now as I type this page. I still recall that first self-declaration of being an artist.

I was drawing as a child before I could even recite or write the alphabet. One of my first inspirations as this young child was Captain Bob. He had a morning show where he would draw and tell stories with his drawings. My greatest inspiration was my sister Cheryl all through my school years she'd show me how to improve my drawings. As we grew older through our youth we even did creative projects together for Christmas.

My Brother Jim would draw when I'd ask him to draw me a train or a submarine.

Yep, I was an artist as a child and didn't realize it. All I ever heard was from other people was: "One day you'll be and artist," or "If you work real hard in school and college you could become and artist," and the one I hated the most was, "The life of an artist is tough look into becoming something else!"

Somewhere in life I stopped believing even though I did have those people and friends that believed in me. I chose to listen to the negativity instead of the positive, myself, and what came naturally . . . I do wonder what would have happened if I pursued art instead of the Navy? Now I wouldn't want to change, the out come, I love my children. I wonder that's all.

Ever wonder if we are the reflection and whatever goes on inside the mirror is the reality? Do we only mimic our counter part through the looking glass? Our dreams are their dreams. We really have no say in life because; life is but a dream . . . Hmmm.

Alice has entered the other side. I'm sure she can tell us what we want to know! To think that bunny rabbits really do talk, there are men and women cards that rule and serve, and maybe twiddle Dumb and twiddle Dee are really rocket scientist. So, if you stare into the mirror to long, you may see something that you never wanted too. Gazers beware when holding a mirror and you are marveling at self. What if self (what you think is the reflection) said, "Enough? Put the mirror down, and run away. I've seen enough!"

If you drop the mirror you will have 7 years of misery if you believe in superstition. If you don't believe in misery after you dropped and broken the mirror please be careful cleaning up the mess. You wouldn't want to cut yourself. When you break a mirror and star into the pieces on the floor do you see one scattered reflection or hundreds of tiny ones? Perhaps your reflection is laughing at you so don't freak out. Why is your reflection (so you think) laughing at you. Why you just release his/her spirit into your world. Now the spirit can travel from both worlds freely at any time or to any place. Sleep well at night. I'm sure your counterpart is . . .

Maybe a broken mirror mosaic would be an interesting art project. See, something good can come out of a smashed mirror.

Outta Sbzzz Mind   by Sb Waitt

Who is that man in the mirror?

BE CAREFUL WHEN YOU TAKE YOUR TRASH TO THE ALLEY AND DUMP IT INTO S TRASH CAN YOU NEVER KNOW WHEN YOU'LL RUN INTO AN ALLEYGATOR

ALLEYGATORS HAVE AN EXOSKELETON SKULL that is very hard! Through, the recent and fast evolutiontionary process of the evolving current day and/or night alligator into a keen, intelligent, and sophisticated animal. YES I said sophisticated and intelligent! They have read several discarded books about Darwin and his theories as well as numerous books on: philosophy, physiology, and Physics (They have a thing about books beginning with the letter "P." Rumor has it they meet-up for weekly discussion on the current book of the month . . . They are also dipping into the classics such as Kipling, Hemingway, Descartes', Poe, Swift, Henway and the list goes on!

Anyway getting back to the physical development of the Alleygator . . . They have developed an exceptionally hard cranium due to the various things, objects and pieces of junk that could and do fall upon there head. Maybe now you'll be a little neater about tossing your old unwanted stuff into the vicinity of the trash cans. Your uncaringness, laziness, and untidiness caused this evolutionary process. Are we going to have to live with this situation of un-gargantuan proportions? I say, "Je ne Sais pas."

Some of the pet alligators that were flushed down the toilet migrated out of the sewer system into the alleyways, in people's yards, and dumpsters. They found it was a safer environment. Food wise they are selective about garbage however. What attracts them is there is a high volume of cats, dogs, rats, birds, etc . . . that like to rummage around the trash cans. Not to mention a tasty finger, hand or foot from those not paying attention to what's going on around themselves, while haphazardly throwing away their refuge before trash day. How often in our past have we been told, "Be aware, pay attention, hold your head up, don't slouch, eat your vegetables, people are starving . . . well you know what I'm saying."

They are very quick, hard to catch, and developed a stronger jaw than the typical gator found in the wild. They must not exceed the length of 4 feet. Why you ask? Because, once over 4 feet in length they are considered a nuisances by Pest Control Authority. Pest control will only stop by and attempt to catch them from your land if sited and reported by residents in the neighborhood.

One other development you may not know about them is their ability to mimic the sounds of other animals, nature, and humans. It may not be long before you hear the words to the effect of, "Hey dad can you come out here and help me!" Too bad, so sad, Dad wasn't all that bad, the gator is glad, cause he just had, dad . . . Are you mad, dad was rad, and he has now been had . . .

On the plus side, the alleygators keep strangers from using your cans or camping out if you have an awning or some kind of protection over your trash area. Keep your trash protected you never know who will want to steal your trash and write a story about all the garbage you throw out. One mans garbage is another man's treasure, fortune, or just more junk for his junk room, as the saying goes. You know the saying . . . Good enough.

One night, at my house, I heard something outside around the trash. It was a family of raccoons. They are brazen suckers! They didn't budge an inch . . . The little children kept eating as momma stood up and looked at me. She clicked out something in raccoon talk so the little ones would keep munching without fear. I clicked off the flashlight and went in the house. I could of sworn on of them critters was asking me to toss out some ketchup, or was it hot sauce? Our neighborhood was terrorized by one raccoon a few years ago. They can cause a lot of destruction to shake roofs. Anyway, he'd/she'd come up to my back sliding door and knock on the window as if to say, "You can't catch me, kneenier, kneenier kneenier!"

Now if we all had alleygators around our trash the raccoons wouldn't have come around anymore after the first member of the clan did some yelling from the belly of an Alleygator. My neighbor use to have a fish pond in his backyard. It was a fish pond by day and a raccoon feeder by night. Same goes for bird feeder by day and rat feeder at night.

Now alligators may never replace your dog. They may come to an understanding with you over a period of time. So the possibility, this is where mutual respect could come into play. From his/her perspective; "If you allow me to live in peace, while providing food . . . I won't bit your hand or leg and I'll keep all the yummy pests away from your yard." Yea, man and beast co-operating together in the wilds of your yard! My back yard is like a jungle in the spring time after all the rains.

Oh yea for those of you that don't know a hen weighs about 1 ½ to 2 pounds . . . remember, "Henway?"

Outta Sbzzz Mind by Sb Waitt

Beware of alleygators

A BATTLE LANTERN

ON BOARD NAVY SHIPS THERE were these lanterns or flashlight devices mounted to the bulkhead of every compartment (bulkheads are walls on board ships.) When power would shut off, whether intentional or not, the battle lantern would energize and light the path to overcome darkness. One can safely move about the ship to help restore power or go where ever help is needed. There are no portholes (windows) below the main deck of a ship and it gets dark without artificial lighting. Hopefully, the Damage Control Petty Officer performed the planed maintenance in accordance to the PMS card . . . There's a check that the DCPO is suppose to do that checks the battery so it will work when needed to. Of course navy batteries are not always reliable at times, especially, if they were stored in a warm storage locker. Some of us would carry a mag light or pin light flashlight with us for extra protection. We'd never know when the lights would go out and be fumbling around in the dark.

While aboard USS Gray FF 1054 a frigate out of San Diego California. Did you know there is more than one city called San Diego in the United States . . . ? Ha ha, gotchya . . . Well maybe not. There is a San Diego Texas, where else is there a city named San Diego in the United States?

Anyway back to the last train of thought before I boarded the train to La la land. I drew a sketch or two of one of these lanterns and let my fantasy world take over. I would imagine them with capabilities of flight. Another time their light would become a lazar beam, an incinerator ray, or a transporter in rescue ("Scotty, beam me up!") or a death ray to intruders. Then one day I saw arms sprouting out of the side and they would pick up the fire axe, spear, mace or some other implement of destruction. The eye in the front would be linked into a micro-positronic brain that would give it cognitive recognition capabilities so it would know who was or was not part of the crew.

Battle lanterns of the future will have no limits. They will be crucial, indispensable, and vital in the support and aid to the ship and crew of the naval ship. Soon one day a version will be created for home, office, work and our car.

The civilian Battle lantern will truly be affective in combating fire and theft; providing thier intelligence is limited so that a terminator world doesn't happen. We wouldn't want to be dominated by battle lanterns. Waiting for their power to run down will not be effective. They have arms remember? So they can repair each other. I'm sure with terminator intelligence it wouldn't be long before the Battle Lantern start to redesign themselves with better power sources. Soon to follow would be enhanced defensive and offensive upgrades making the independent device stronger and harder to defeat. What, it has no feet you say, well that might be the next upgrade. They may determine that there are times when feet and legs have an advantage over flight, perhaps that design will conserve energy. It's all about energy. He with the most energy will win.

I was talking to one of my buddies that are currently serving on active duty in the navy today. He said the only difference is the light bulb in the front has been converted to LED's.

I wonder if a battle lantern could be turned into a video game. If it is, I'd like it in the style of the original Doom, Serious Sam, or Redneck Rampage. I like the first person, shoot-em'-up style of games. Maybe a few of the, "find the hidden compartment and items one needs on the way," type of stuff. I like these games, cause they are not to complicated. Doesn't require a lot of thought, there is a little hand-eye coordination, and best of all . . . I find them fun, even though they can be a little crass. It's all a reflection! Yes I can be a little crass from time to time. I do have character defects that pop up from time to time and get in the way of being personable, friendly, nice, or something like that. Maybe it's called being human.

So the next time you turn on the hallway light or a lamp by your bed be glad it's not a battle lantern that is lighting up your rooms for light at night.

Outta Sbzzz Mind   by Sb Waitt

A Battle Lantern

WANTING THE UPPER HAND . . .

BE CAREFUL WHAT YOU ASK for, you might get it!

He wanders off from his party of archeologist and discoverers an opening in the hillside. Slowly he walks in. "It's a cave," he thinks to himself! He wandered cautiously deeper and deeper into the cave and found some old artifacts. "Wow, a lamp! Maybe I can rub the lamp and a genie will appear," he said out loud with laughter. The explorer bends down and picks up the lamp. His eyes widened as he inspected the outside of the old relic. His hands felt how smooth the lamp was to the touch. The thought and urge overpowered him. He began to rub and rub the lamp and said with a smirk, "Oh genie of the lamp, I command you to appear!"

As smoke billowed out of the lamp, he dropped it on to the sandy floor of the cave. The smoke swirled and turned until a vaporistic shape of an apparition began to appear. At first it was translucent and then the mass of vapor slowly took on humanistic looking form through the apparent transformation. He could now see a strong muscular male genie floating in the air with a tail anchored from the spout of the lamp. Then the words deep, rich and strong echoed though the cave, "Master, your wish is my command . . . I shall grant you 3 wishes."

"Ahhh, waa wa waaa what?" he replied.

Then again, "Master, your wish is my command . . . I shall grant you 3 wishes."

"Who are you?"

"I am the host of the magic lamp. I am a Gen. Until I protect this vessel from unworthy souls for one thousand years, I am destined to stay imprisoned to the lamp."

"Why are you in the lamp?"

"I was wrongly accused and sentenced to perform just deeds in the name of my Master the king of the Arabian Dessert. I was falsely captured to protect the identity of the true thief of the king; his right-hand man, the leader and captain of his royal army." He paused and continued, "If you use one of your wishes on me, to let me go free . . . This too will break the attachment and sentence to me and the lamp. It is a gesture of kindness which will release all Gens or Jennies from the punishment for stealing. On this kind act I will be indebted to you for life. I will forever be your friend. So, again I say, "Master, your wish is my command . . . I shall grant you 3 wishes.""

A smile grew wide after a short period of deep thought. He replies with authority, "I want to be twice as smart as everyone else and always have the upper hand in life so I may always be successful, wealthy and happy."

The Gen crosses his muscular arms, closes his eyes briefly and then responds with, "Your wish is my command!"

Interesting way of life . . . two heads, one big hand, and big feet for balance. I guess it depends on whether your right or left headed and then the question is, which head is the dominate one? A thought occurred about the hand. The thumb could be on the right or left as well. I wonder if it's in conflict or harmony with the dominate head? No changing of the hand if your parent's doesn't want you to be a south paw. It is what it is!

When sitting in a restaurant waiting for the drinks to come. Will the waiter or waitress bring you two straws automatically or will you have to ask for two? Hmmmmmmmmmm. Perhaps she'll carry out two drinks with one straw in each glass. And the next question is . . . Will I be charged for two glasses?

So you must be wondering did he use up all his wishes and did the Gen go free? Your thinking, well, he didn't change into something else so he must have used up all his wishes . . . Only time will tell and it is not up to me to say one way or another; seems like when I ask questions all I do is talk to the hand anyway.

Outta Sbzzz Mind   by Sb Waitt

Beware what you ask for!

"YOU'RE ONCE, TWICE, THREE TIMES A LADY"

I'VE ENJOYED LISTENING TO THIS song over the years and even more now since I drew this picture. Lionel Richie has a smooth wonderful and appealing voice to me.

I was never one for dancing. In grade school we were forced to square dance. There were more boys than girls so some of us use to sit out a dance. The way we came back in was by the teacher making the switch or a girl tagging us on the side line. Unfortunately, I was always tagged. The first time I danced on my own was overseas in the Philippines around the 1977 time frame. The town of Olongapo was just outside of the Subic Bay Naval Base. The main strip was wall to wall bars, night clubs, restaurants, bar-b-q shacks and food carts on the street. After work when liberty-call went down. We'd hit the beach as we'd say. Yep, another fun evening of bar hopping; now I was not a drinker of alcohol so I always drank soda. The soda over there was ok if it was a main name brand, however there was a soda called "Jolly time." Arggg it was not a refreshing drink and it didn't taste that good either.

In the night clubs there was always a live band playing music. These bands mimicked the real band very well. Occasionally there was a word or two that was mispronounced, however for the most part they were great to listen too. After hoping around to a few clubs this one girl comes over to our table, grabs me and pulls me to the dance floor. I said, "I don't dance." She held on and said, "Take it easy, have fun, nobody cares how you dance." So after that club I danced willingly in just about every club I came too.

Near the end of the night as curfew set in for all sailors to be off the streets. The song "Freebird" by Lynyrd Skynyrd would kick in and play. This one song I believe I remember the most. Even today when I hear this song I think about dancing over seas.

What's funny is I only danced in Olongapo for fun. My ship pulled into Freemantle Australia and a bunch of us went out night clubbing. I danced once and felt so out of place. I wonder if that girl ever got over me not wanting to continue dancing. The music ended and I said, "That's it."

Near the end of the deployment we made one last stop in Subic Bay before crossing the Pacific to go home. At liberty call, a group of us waited for one another, gathered together, and ventured into town for the last night of partying.

After the last dance we'd be hungry. There was lots of great food in town to munch on. Now there was these meat sticks. The people at the stands cooking them called them Bar-B-Q's. They were stacked a mile high on the hibachis. We, the sailors called the meat sticks, "monkey meat." Didn't know what kind of meat it was, didn't want to know. They were cheap and tasted good. More Good stuff to eat is the lumpia and pansit. One can never eat enough lumpia and pansit!

The next time I danced was with my mother at my buddies wedding. I was never one to sit down and work on one project at a time . . .

Like I mentioned . . . I like to mix things up a bit. I keep moving the pictures around figuring out which to place in this first book. Sometimes I find it hard to build a brick wall because one usually assembles the wall one brick at a time. I want to do it all at once. I'm good at complicating things so this current project isn't any different from my standard mode of operation.

Back to the dancing . . . Now when I go out and do some dancing it's really fun. I find if I smile and laugh while I'm dancing, the other person will believes I'm having a good time; so, they as well will have a good time. If you or me give them the impression that they are the center of your universe while dancing you/me will almost never go wrong; even if dancing isn't your best forte in life. I have a tough time with the line dancing. It's too much like aerobics and my feet get a bit tangled up on the floor and before I know it . . . I'm on the floor all sprawled out. I do my best to stick with free dancing to rock and roll or an occasional slow dance.

Outta Sbzzz Mind   by Sb Waitt

"You're once, twice, three times a lady"

OCT-O-PANTS

OF COURSE AN OCTOPUS WOULD wear pants with eight legs if he/she was too, hence oct-o-pants. It sort of sounds like the word occupants, so, oct-u-pants would work as well.

The thing I hated the most that I did with my parents was clothes shopping for school. I'd rather be home watching TV or out playing with my friends in the neighborhood.

They'd say, "Here, try this on." Yuck! So I did. They'd ask me, "Do you like it?" I'd say, "Yep, it's great . . . it's wonderful . . . thank you!" I really didn't care what I wore for clothes. Once I didn't wear a t-shirt when clothes shopping. My mother wanted to know the size I was currently wearing so she reaches for my collar to look under it for the t-shirt size. "You're not wearing a T-shirt," she says aloud. Boy I got an ear full that night. I'm looking up at the sky right now an am saying, "I love you Ma."

Now when I started going to school there was a dress code. For boys; pants, button shirt, polo shirt with collar, shoes, etc . . . I always had to wear underwear and T-shirt and white socks . . . I was allowed to wear sneaker for gym day only during elementary school. Once I hit high school we had baskets at the gym for out gym attire.

I remember in 7th grade history class one of my classmates was talking quietly about clothes to one of his friends. He then turned to me and began commenting on the way I dress. He said in a sarcastic tone of voice, "Where do you buy your cool clothes?" I reply, "I didn't buy them or pick them out . . . My mother bought them for me." He began to laugh and said, "Right! Your mother bought them." The truth is, she did. As time went on I didn't go clothes shopping anymore. It was easier for my parents to buy them with out me being there with the exception of shoes. I'm glad I didn't have eight legs.

Speaking of shoes . . . I didn't learn to tie my shoes until 2nd grade. My first grade teacher got tired of tying my shoes so she sent a note home to my parents . . . Shortly after the note I wore loafers to school. Come winter time I wore these rubber boots over my loafers. I'd continually put the wrong boot over the wrong shoe . . . They'd get stuck and were hard to remove. Course I did this at school when it was time to go home. After a few battles with the rubber boots and stuck shoes my teacher solved the problem with another note to my parents . . . I wasn't the teacher's favorite student back then.

So in Junior High School I was picked on most of all about my wearing of white socks. I was called nerd and lots of other soon to be un-politically correct names; things where different back in the 1960's. My buddy across the street talked with my mom one day and told her about the white socks stuff that goes on at school. So that one day I was given black socks to wear for school. I actually put up a fuss about wearing them. However, I went to school that day and the rest of my school life in black socks. I was sitting on my stool in Mr. Raymond's 9th grade science class; waiting for everyone to come in from lunch when Michael walked in. He made a big deal out of what he saw, he was first to say anything aloud, "Look at that! Where'd your white socks go?" If it was such a big deal why'd it take so long for someone to say something that day?

Near the end of my school years growing up; the day was Senior Skip Day, only I didn't skip school. I wore dungarees and sneaker for the first time in my life to school. I went un-noticed in school about the clothes I wore! Why, because, the school dress code hadn't been in existence for about at least 6 years now. The public school system figured out that, what ever children and teens wore to school as long as it covered up private areas, no profanity written on it, and was somewhat respectful was of no concern to the education system.

When I got home from school on senior skip day I got an ear full about what I wore to school; it was so wrong! Again I'm looking up to the sky, "I love ya Ma." Apparently, my parents never got the memo about the change or they didn't agree and I was held hostage in the belief system (most likely the later.) Hmmm, "Oct-u-pants" or "Oct-o-pants?"

by Sb Waitt

Outta Sbzzz Mind

Sbwaitt

Oct-o-pants

15

"I'VE GOT LOCOMOTIVE BREATH!"

ONE OF MY FAVORITE SONGS by Jethro Tull is, "Locomotive Breath!" I always enjoyed the studio version of this song the best until I saw them perform this live in San Diego . . . I still have my ticket stub. I'm one of those that likes to hold on to ticket stubs from concerts, plays, musicals, baseball games, etc . . . etc . . .

So there I am with a locomotive coming out of my mouth in this drawing. I hear the train whistle blasting, smell the smoke funneling out of the stack, and I can hear the screeching sound of steel on steel as the train travels on the curved track for a turn . . . Every time I go to the happiest place on earth and ride one their trains this song comes to mind. I'd really like to hear it while we enter the tunnels.

Some evenings, after a night of eating out at restaurants, I have locomotive breath. I enjoy indulging in new foods, flavors, and spices. I enjoy sushi with wasabi. Before I dunk my sushi in my mixture of soy sauce and wasabi, I ensure it is the right color and hotness. The mixture looks like cloudy coffee in color and appearance. When I dip my sushi, lift the chop sticks to place the delectable tidbit into my mouth and start to chew. I feel a quick rush up the nose, followed by a face flash . . . Then my eye socks start to sizzle and water and then the forehead and the nap of the neck sweats. If I put too much wasabi in with the soy sauce I lose my breath. Losing my breath is not the pleasurable affect that I want to obtain and enjoy.

Do you ever wake-up in the morning with locomotive breath. When married it's a mad dash to the toothbrush and paste. A gargle later you bounce back into bed and say with a smile, "Good morning sweetheart. Did you sleep well?" It's funny when she turns her head away and says, "Yep . . ." She's not admitting to it. However, she has locomotive breath!

Back to trains . . . As a child, occasionally my dad would ask me, "What would you like to do today?" I'd reply, "Go to the Beverly/Salem Bridge and watch the trains." I enjoyed watching the trains on the bridge cross over the river. The train bridge paralleled the car bridge so we'd park the car nearby and walk along the sidewalk towards the center of the bridge. We'd stand and wait for a train. I liked it. We may have only waited for 2 or 3 trains. That was OK with me. I really enjoyed watching when two trains from opposite directions passed on the bridge. In my mind that was the best occurrence.

I had a few train sets as a child. I'd imagine myself as an engineer while playing. I always wanted to pull on the cord that made the train whistle blow! Most likely in today's world there is a button and/or it's all automated.

When watching the Addams family on TV, I was always jealous of Gomez Addams and his train set. I'm not sure I'd want to blow up my trains the way he did. He always had the best looking layout for trains. The whistles would always sound just moments before the explosion. The grin on his face and the twinkle in his eyes, told the story of how much fun he was having. The childhood youth lived every time he touched the controls.

My first long train ride was going to Navy Boot camp at the end of May 1976. The ride was an overnighter with a bed in the sleeper car. I went to sleep that night to the sound of, "Click clack, click clack, click clack." It was better than any music on my stereo. Little did I know at the time, the movement of the train would be similar to the way a ship would rock at sea from small waves during a light breeze?

I'm one of those individuals that like to watch the long freight trains at crossings. I got a hoot out of trains that were over 100 cars long. I saw them a lot when I was stationed in Charleston South Carolina. My Aunt and Uncles house in Charlestown Massachusetts ran along a street with elevated subway trains. They made a high pitch squeal sound while traveling on the curved parts of the track. I use to sit by the window on the second floor and watch the trains for hours, it never got old.

Outta Sbzzz Mind

by SbWaitt

"I've got locomotive breath!"

SALLY WOKE UP AND WAS
A STATUE ON EASTER ISLAND

SOMETIMES IN A DREAM WE wake-up and wonder, "Where am I?" Only, what if you woke up and it wasn't a dream? The alarm never goes off, the cat doesn't sit on your head to wake you up for food, the cell phone never rings, or the trash trucks don't bang the cans, make noise and you open your eyes suddenly and scream aloud in panic, "It's trash day!" So, you make a mad dash panic to the cans while half dressed to push them to the street before it's too late. Aaaa, ya missed it. So you attempt to run down the street with one can to no avail while, yelling, "Stop, stop!"! I'm sure the guy driving is looking at his side rear view mirror laughing and wondering, "How far can I drive away down the street before he stops following me?"

Back to, "Where am I?" What if? You're conscious of being in a strange place. You have a new view. Your head doesn't turn in any direction. Screaming doesn't work. This dream goes on and on and on and on, before you believe you're in the worse nightmare you've ever been in. This nightmare seems as if it goes on and on forever. "Huh?" You keep thinking any minute now and I'll wake up, I'll open my eyes, and the cat will fiddle with my toes because she's hungry and wants to be served.

Nope! Night and day go by the same scenery with the exception of night and day, weather, or an occasional on looker that comes to the island to visit and explore. That last sight of a human being one will drive you nuts. Because, no matter how hard you strive to communicate, nothing comes out of your mouth. Hmmmm, maybe the birds will be the one that drives you nuts the most; because, birds do what birds do and they do it anywhere the moment strikes them to do-do it! And it usually strikes you.

I don't know if you'll ever feel itchy and are unable to scratch or if a crack develops and you'll feel pain. I don't know if when an animal or insect walks across your stone base or something lands in your eye if you will feel there presents physically either? I don't know if you'll ever experience happiness again?

I do imagine, one day, years latter; you may hear a vice and wonder, "That voice sounds so familiar!" and the face comes into view and it's you staring at you. Only you are no longer you. She is you and maybe I am she. If you could, I believe you would cry because I'm sure she is. I see tears rolling down her face.

Then, after visual contact, you wonder what hell did she go through all these years before arriving at the island? Where you too a stone head is fixed to the ground? If she touches me will we revert back to the way it was? Will I now wake up or will she walk away and I will continue to be a statue? She touches you and you now know it's a hopeless place to be. Yep, it's like a scene you might watch out of an old twilight zone show! Any moment you'll hear the narration of Rod Sterling. You never hear the voice and the nightmare continues

Perhaps, before she leaves; you will develop a tear from your eye and you'll stare at one another for a few more moments as she leaves? You never have that moment because she is already walking away. "Wait!" you attempt to scream aloud but it is only to yourself! Again another effort to yell, "Don't go! Please tell me what is going on!" Yet, she keeps on walking away. As you see her in the distance for one last moment before she steps out of view. You think to yourself, "Will I ever see her again? What if I do? How much longer will I have to endure this insane existence? Will I ever stop being and die?

Perhaps one day many, many years latter. You'll wake up and find you're not a stone head statue on a remote Island in the Pacific ocean anymore . . . Your time has come. You now possess another person's body. This processes, experience, mind transformation, or what ever you want to call it, has been going on for thousands of years. Perhaps it's not just the one statue head or limited to this island? This could be going on all over the world.

So you wake up from a dream and go to the bathroom sink to dampen a washcloth to wipe your face. You look up into the mirror at your reflection, you say, "who are you?" You turn your head and wonder whose life am I living? Now you say out loud, "No way? That didn't just happen? I was dreaming!" Yet you have a feeling and inkling. You're compelled to go and seek what has happened. A new madness has begun. I am still a stranger to myself. As your dreams reoccur over and over as the restless nights turn into day. You find you're on a quest for truth.

And that day when you finally make contact with the stone head, as your counterpart did before you . . . It is as if it all never happened. You are who you are and never were you someone else or a stone statue standing still. Because, once you touched the statue your mind quickly starts to erase that which happened . . . Your hell is over. The though, "Life is good," comes to mind! You think to yourself, "I always wanted to go to Easter Island?" Where too next you think with a smile? Happiness has returned.

Outta Sbzzz Mind   by Sb Waitt

One morning Sally woke up and was a statue on Easter Island

RADISH PEOPLE
ARE MUSICALLY INCLINED

ONE OF MY FAVORITE FORMS of entertainment is to go to a coffee house, specially if there is live entertainment . . . Dead entertainment is so boring. I like to go when I know there is an open mike night. A variety of people will go on stage to perform and express themselves. When they are on stage they are the best of what is being done at the moment. If you don't like it leave or get on stage yourself. No booing! They are doing what you may have dreamed of doing . . . Performing! Singing publically! Expressing one's self!

I likes to doodle in a book of blank pages while people sing, play music, or recite poetry it excites my brain. The thoughts flow and before I know it my brain is moving the pen in hand. Sometimes it's a written though about a future cartoon and other times it's coming out as a sketch . . . I've sketched a few performers from time to time. If a girl sounds like an angel I'll add a pair of wings, if someone sounds earthy to me they'll be in bare feet with vines growing up the microphone stand, if they are hot; they may have horns, a tail, and fire all around them, and sometimes I'll draw something about the song as part of the background. The possibilities are endless . . .

Many an evening at a coffee shop I've written stories, worked on my homework, as well as draw. Others times I go to socialize, drink more coffee than needed, enjoy the entertainment, relax and have fun. It's always fun to walk away with a new friend or go out afterwards for breakfast late at night with the gang.

I likes being in a friendly environment the most, the creative process flows out easy onto the paper. Thoughts do come out in other environments; usually they come out afterwards when I'm in a safe place. Time spent or enjoyed is better when it is fun and safe to me. Some things are beyond my control so I do my best to have an out and leave when I've had enough of a not so good thing to me.

I'm sometimes where I am and may not want to be (May not be my first or second choice) is because I trust those I am with. Life is give and take. I acknowledge those I went out with before I leave and thank them for the invite. Just because I'm ready to go or had enough does not mean what is going on is a bad thing. It only means I'm ready to go, till next time, take good care, look forward in going out with yaz again, bye, see ya later, Yak yak yak, bla bla blaaa, etc . . .

I believe this cartoon is a reflection of me because I've always wanted the gift of song. I hear my voice like that of a squeaky, squawky, wheel when I talk. I have a piano that I make noise on and on occasion even make music with. To play with a band at Carnegie hall is a dream. Karaoke is a once in a while thing I do with friends from time to time. No pressure with lots of fun.

At a stop lights if you look at me behind the wheel I'm usually bellowing out a song whilst driving, well at the light stopping, stopped, idling. Only occasion when I'm in the shower do I sing, heavy on the occasion part. It sounds more like gargling then singing.

I don't imagine radish people like hanging out at taco stands. The condiments usually include: spicy carrots with onions and jalapeños, salsa, and radishes. When I've crossed the border and ventured into Mexico with friends, I ate lots of radishes. Good eats down there. Some foods I eat and don't ask questions. There's this black sauce called mole' Mmm mm tasty! On the way across the border returning to the USA we are asked if we have anything to declare. I usually declare, "Indigestion from all food!" I get a smile or two from my comments. Now that I thinks of it . . . Eating at some of the taco stands in TJ may not be the smartest thing to do . . . Specially munching on the raw vegetables; because, where and how they grow them nobody knows . . .

Something that is nice about radish people is they are very laid back. Very little bothers them. They are very happy, love to give and receive hugs and are very creative. I've found as time goes on I can never have enough radish people friends . . .

Outta Sbzzz Mind
by Sb Waitt

Radish people are musically inclined

GAS PUMP GIRL

ONLY THE BEST GAS FOR these women and their shoes. When you have big feet one must take extra good care of them. That's the shoes and feet I'm talking about. The expense is a factor; however, 'Gas Pump Girls' use high test seeing as they are constantly on the go. No stopping them once they have their mind set . . . they become very goal orientated. So until their personal mission is accomplished its go, go, go and push, push, push! They possess an unending drive until satisfaction is achieved. They're smart, intelligent, like to have fun and enjoy fast cars. Oh yes dancing is high on their list of fun things to do.

I likes high heels. I like to look at the various designs, especial black and shiny. I like they way they sound on wood, tile, pavement and numerous other surfaces. I like what they do to the appearance and shape of women's legs. Throw in a pair of jet black panty hose and you have me eating out of the palm of your hand, maybe even eating out of your shoe . . . If, you're a women that is. High heels shoes look good on you when you're dressed up to the nines, while you're wearing jeans, or you're in your grubbiest of grubbies.

I believe you have the right to wear or not wear heels. After all, your feet belong to you and you alone not your boss at work. It's a package deal with the body. So if you want to wear sneakers at work or a formal event then, by all means, you have that right. Be kind to your feet and be kind to the rest of yourself. If you don't walk in them please consider wearing them once you sit down. Oh yea, and do that thing where you dangle your shoe and rock it up and down.

You may not have to walk in high heels however, if a girl wears them and is on the couch sitting next to me, you may receive a foot rub from time to time or as many times as you wear the pumps. Yep I likes to give women foot rubs. I'll give them anywhere and any place. I've given foot massages at baseball games, movies, restaurants, in the park, in the car, etc . . . I likes to give them not receive them. I am ticklish, very ticklish . . . It's a curse!

I like to over exaggerate the feet on some of my cartoons. On the women they are usually in over size heels that fit their big feet and the men will have feet so big that they are not wearing shoes. Finding shoes to match your feet is difficult in real life. I wear extra wide shoes and my right foot is almost a half size larger. I've twisted my right foot and ankle religiously every year since first grade. My right foot is a bit messed up. My parachuting accident in 1979 didn't help any. When I landed, it felt as if like the top of my foot bent to the front of my leg. I hobbled for about 3 months.

My last accident the doctor asked my when I broke my foot and said it was calcified. I said I never broke my foot that I know of. I guess I question the ability of some of my past doctors in reading X-rays. Doctors are human and make mistakes.

Ok, ok back to the big feet on men and women. I'm the artist. I can draw shoes for them if I want too. However, I don't always want too. You have the option of picking up a pen, pencil or brush and designing some if you like.

Maybe one day astronauts will land on planet where everyone has big feet. They'd be stable and hard to knock over, kind of like Weebles, they wobble but don't fall down. Weebbles was a toy during my youth, look it up on the computer. Course only if you want too. I'm not telling you what to do.

Alright back on this newly discovered world that's inhabited by large foot beings; I wonder what they would call their equivalent of big foot and how much bigger would their feet be? "Stomp foot, thunder foot, or quake foot" perhaps? Playing hop scotch, jump rope, and three legged races would be interesting. What do ya think about playing a game of twister?

Do you know why Gas Pump Girls like fast cars . . . ? They have heavy feet. So when they have the opportunity to drive. The car must; look hot and shiny, be a convertible, have a great sound system, and it must supplement their eyes and hair. Hey, a little vanity is good for self-ego and esteem at times. They like to be stopped by both male and female police officers.

Outta Sbzzz Mind   by Sb Waitt

Gas Pump Girl

BABY TOILET TRAINING

"COME ON, JUMP TOILET JUMP . . . jump toilet jump!" Do ya think an intelligent child could teach a toilet how to jump? Does this thought come to mind when you think about toilet training a baby? It has for me.

My brother Jim and his wife Louise lived in Calimesa California about 20 minutes or so east of the Riverside/San Bernardino area. I was up from San Diego to visit for the weekend and one Saturday afternoon I was asked if I could watch one of their friends children while they all took off to run a few earns. I've baby sat children from time to time over the years, so I figured it wouldn't be any problem. I find children are usually fun. I've been are around them before . . . So I didn't think there would be any problem.

The youngest child, a small toddler boy was in the process of toilet training through the day and what do know? He had to use the bathroom. Now I was taught many moons ago to place small boy children on the toilet backwards. This gives them something to hold onto whilst they do what they need to do. You know, make bubbles, poop, play with the toilet paper, and make funny sounds.

This small child went a couple of times while I was watching the little critter. I think he like the idea of sitting on the toilet backwards. This way, it's not so scary; because, the seat does not fall upon you when you're a boy. That has to hurt when the seat drops and slams, crunches, or pinches the boy's little bubble maker, ouch. So sitting on the toilet backwards, was a fun and safe game to him. I believe he really only had to go the first time. All the other trips to the bathroom were entertaining to himself.

Later in the afternoon, all earns where accomplished by the grown-ups and my duty as baby sitter was over. I never gave it another thought about telling his mom how many times he went to the bathroom and how many times he actually did something in the toilet.

The next time I came up to visit from San Diego, I was asked if I knew why he liked to sit on the toilet backwards. Of course I knew why. I assumed all parents taught their children that this is how you do it. At least he didn't fall into the toilet or have another type of casualty.

So from that day forward, if the child I watched didn't have their own personal potty chair, I asked the parents how the child was to sit upon the toilet. They'd look at me and laugh and would reply, "How do you think they sit on the toilet seat?" So I'd drop it and let it go at that . . . That is, the words of the parents that is not the toilet seat.

That word toilet, in my home, was not spoken. I know I used the word "hopper" in its place. The spoken word "toilet" was vulgar as expressed to me by my mother, when I was a child. At least it was in my home for me growing up. I remember yelling out, "Hey Dad . . . The hopper is stopped up again." I don't ever remember my dad explaining to me about the use of a plunger or telling me I used to much paper? The toilets back then had a better "Koowoosh" sound to it! They probably weren't as water conscious back then.

When I was a smaller child I remember my mom always wanted to check me after I sat on the hopper. Guess I was lazy and didn't wipe very good. The last time she ever checked me was the day she had a bunch of her lady friends over. I yelled out, "Hey Mom, come and check me." Yep that was the last time. Perhaps, I embarrassed her that day? We start out in diapers, become toilet trained and all goes well till we hit a golden age when some of us return to diapers. I'm not there yet however we don't know what tomorrow will hold for us. You know . . . ? Some good here, a little bad there, diapers oh the sink, but if all goes well . . . possibly, perhaps a little baklava?

I think embarrassment is over rated. You can see how worried I am about embarrassment after reading about my last time being checked while sitting on the hopper. I think we use the embarrassment word because we no longer have control in particular situations. I'm not saying that it would nice if people talked only about their business. Hey, we're human; we make mistakes, put our foot in our mouths and pray for forgiveness.

Outta Sbzzz Mind   by Sb Waitt

A baby toilet training

IN A CLONE WORLD OF JAY LENO

WOULD JAY LENO FIND HIMSELF funny in a clone world? What would humor be like in a clone world? You, I, me would be the butt of all jokes.

What if we lived in a clone world where everyone looked a like? Being "unique" would be very difficult. Would it even be part of the vocabulary? I'm sure it would, maybe . . . I'll think about that some more. After all there are twins, triplets and such born into the world and they turn out different. Even with all their similarities they are different.

In the clone world will . . . all males and females look alike and that goes for the children too . . . Yes even the children, hmmm. When they grow up and have babies, their babies are identical. They all age the same. Is it possible to have a clone world so perfect that the cells don't breakdown, mutate and cause differences with each generation. I believe if we can think of it, it can happen. Course there will be those male and female differences.

Perhaps the only differences would be from body marks, changing the hair color and style, nail coloring, or type of clothing. The possibility of a world like this without clothing could happen. Maybe the voice is slightly different? There are different thoughts and ideas from person to person. With all the stars and possible planets out there, what are the possible combinations for life to be totally alike and/or similar in appearance?

If they lived in a collective mind society even their thoughts could be similarly the same. Hmmm, could there be a world of everyone is totally the same in every degree?

We all have a perception of how cloning works, however it's not in existence openly if it's happening today. Science is constantly changing our world and not always for the better. When I talk about cloning . . . I mean to clone someone from a cell and grow them to the desired age of existence . . . Not just clone a cell and implant it and let it grow inside the womb of and animal . . . Clone me today and tomorrow or next week I have a twin walking around with all my memories up to the point of the day of cloning. Once my twin is alive and breathing, he will have new experiences, thoughts, ideas, outlooks, etc . . .

When we look at bugs and insects from our point of view, they mostly all look alike; with the exception of missing a leg, a bite taken out of there body, or have a bent antenna. How different do ants look to each other? Can a worm tell one another apart? Does individuality even matter in the bug and insect kingdom? Lobsters and fish to me are hard to tell apart within their own kind.

Everywhere you go, there you are. No escaping yourself. Would you say to someone, "I don't know if I can trust you, I don't like the way you look?" or how about, "Gee, you look reliable I believe I can trust you?" When you look in a mirror what do you see? In the men's room when you're done combing your hair are you going to ask, "Hey buddy (Jim, Bill, George or whoever,) how do I look? Do you think my girl will find me . . . likeable?" I wonder what excuse a girl would use when you ask her to dance and she's interested in someone else?

Pat Benatar sings a song called, "My Clone Sleeps Alone." Great voice! I've wanted to play this at my wedding along with, "I want a lover that won't drive me crazy."

There are times I wished I had a clone of myself. I think of all the things I/we could do and accomplish. Hey, isn't there a movie about this idea?

It is good we are not clones of one another. Yes we have similarities. At time we see our mirrored reflection in people, however. 'I am me and you are you and together we make weeeee!." I believe this is a saying out there somewhere as well. It's more fun sharing our uniqueness's together in life. With time, we blend in a bit and we still maintain our individuality. I am an individual and that makes me unique. Not to be confused with being a eunuch.

Plus side of a clone world could be . . . No prejudices within the society, peer pressure, why do you have to be different from everyone else, or I don't think you look good in that suite . . . I religion, if there was a verse about being created in His image . . . It definitely would apply.

My friend said to me, "I can't wait to see what the Statue of Liberty looks like . . ." Hmmm, would there be a problem with freedom, liberty, unification, harmony, togetherness, love, etc . . .

Would someone come up with the Idea to create individuality and explore genetics to create differences? Will they think to be different is a third eye, maybe four arms, or big feet. Could, would, will the thought about crating different facial features come to mind? Would there be a clone war?

Well, what do you think? What would your clone world be like?

Outta *Sbzzz Mind*

by Sb Waitt

What Mount Rushmore would look like in a clone world of Jay Leno

OUT OF THE VORTEX AT NIGHT

HOW WELL DO YOU SLEEP at night? Do you feel safe in the dark? What goes on once the eyes are closed tight and the mind is at rest? If you positioned a camera towards you, for recording night time, what activities will happen around your bed? What would you see when you press the playback button? Do you even want to think about this? All is safe until we close our eyes.

A vortex could appear at any given moment in time. Is it a two way opening? Who knows what mysterious creatures will crawl, walk, fall, or fly out? Perhaps the vortex is your mirror? Maybe things come out of your mirror from another dimension once you leave your room? Do you believe that the mirror is an opening to and from a strange world? Hmm, wouldn't you like to be able to see what is just out of view while staring into a mirror? Have you ever attempted to see around the corner in the mirror? Maybe there is something right behind your head out of view . . . if you are by yourself you will never know!

I use to hate going to the bathroom at night as a child. There was always a night light on at night in the bathroom, because bright lights are rude at night. I never wanted to leave the safety of my blanket pulled over my head to go pee. I knew, if I went into the bathroom and looked in the mirror . . . life as I knew it would be over. If I looked into the mirror, I was sure that the last thing I would ever see would be a face behind me, grinning with eyes wide and wild! If I turned real fast out of fear in the effort to defend myself, something would then reach out from the mirror and pull me in! I was doomed . . . I ran in fast and did my business, washed my hands, and ran back to bed as fast as I could . . . Never look into the mirror at night. That was my rule of survival in my house growing up. And you know what . . . ? It still is.

My bedroom while growing up was on the second floor. My house creaked at night and we had radiators that would snap. The floors squeaked and squawked when you walked on them. The windows rattled on breezy nights. Things definitely went bump in the night! To me, the only thing worse and scarier that the upstairs was the thought and act of walking or running into the cellar; don't ever go into the cellar! "Running into and out of," was my typical and standard mode of operation for doing whatever business I was to conduct with the cellar! I didn't even have to go down there to be frightened, as I said . . . thinking about the cellar did me in! I didn't like going down there in the day time even with someone in the house to hear me. And especially at night when I was alone I didn't like going down there.

I'm sure the vortex exists; so beware, be cautious, and be safe. Your being watched even now, in the-what you believe is "safe confines" of your home, car, favorite place to sit and read! As you stare in your TV . . . Do you know for sure what is above your shoulder, out of sight, and ready to attack? The vortex can be a one sided opening at times (kind of like a one way mirror.) Those living things are looking through and waiting for the right moment to come through.

The TV or computer monitor could be a vortex. When you shut if off or turn away . . . You better run. It's always wise to have an exit strategy in mind. Make sure your path is free of obstacles. However, there is no guarantee something will block your path or move the obstruction back in place so you will trip and fall.

So the next time you feel like you are being watched, you are! How about all those times you felt something touch you even when no one is near or how about those things in your room that mysteriously move around? You know, that jar of marbles that ends up on the floor and you trip over it from time to time? The doll that you left on the chair is now at the foot of your bed? Or chair that has been moved sideways out of place. How do you justify or explain the unknown things that you don't want to think about; because, what would the true answer to the strange occurrences mean? You know what it means! You think as long as you don't admit it . . . It's not happening, all is safe, it's just a stray thought I have to scare myself . . . Denial may not be a safe place to be . . . perhaps the next page in this book is a vortex??? Do you know??? Are you safe???

Outta Sbzzz Mind

by Sb Waitt

Out of the vortex of the night your nightmares become reality

MANS' GREATEST INVENTION

YES THIS IS MAN'S GREATEST invention, a square roll of toilet paper. It doesn't fall of the roll when you sit it on the round holder. And, if it does fall off it doesn't roll away from you while sitting on the toilet after it hits the floor.

I believe (not replacing the toilet paper onto the roll) is right up there with not closing the toilet seat after "we" men pee in the toilet. I never remember which, is the proper, way to put the roll of toilet paper onto the holder, anyway. Let's see, is the paper supposed to roll off towards the wall or away from the wall? Does it really matter which way it goes on to the roll? Being single, I don't remember the last time I did put the roll onto the holder. Occasionally after company leaves the roll mysteriously appears on to the holder. Was this done by a man or a woman?

Are you a warder, folder, or a stuffer? What you have no idea what I'm talking about? Ok, here goes. A warder is where you wrap the toilet paper in a big gob around your fingers before wiping. If, you are a folder; you will neatly fold the paper in your hand before usage. So if you are a stuffer; that's where you stuff a bunch of paper in the cup of your hand before you knock the brown stuff off your bottom. I believe folding takes way too much time . . . I want to get in there and out of there as fast as I can. So I usually stuff or wad depending on how easy the paper tears.

I have a buddy that says, "You buy the worse toilet paper!" He complains that it feels like sand paper, I've not used sand paper on my derriere so I wouldn't know. I usually buy single-ply. I never buy scented paper. I can never figure out why anyone would? Maybe it gives the bathroom a fresh aroma afterwards. I've never heard anyone say, "My, you smell good, what scent of toilet paper do you use? Or you stink! Have you considered changing your brand of toilet paper?"

Do you have an animal that likes to eat or play with the roll of toilet paper? I wouldn't want your animal to become sick from the scented paper if you forget to close the door afterwards. I know closing doors isn't one of my fortes, ask my brother Jim.

I remember watching a program on TV about a girl who liked to eat toilet paper. It sounded like it was comforting to her. I don't remember if it was scented or not? As a small child I liked to eat baby cream out of the jar. In school, I enjoyed the taste of the paste we used to stick paper together. I don't know what brand it was or if the paste was made by the teachers from scratch. It was always served on a small square or rectangular piece of paper and we used a Popsicle stick to eat and smear with.

Of course now I'll be thinking about what is woman's greatest invention? Well, it's from the eyes and view of a man. I'll have to ask a woman this question. From my point of view, perhaps . . . ? It's a device that automatically loads the paper onto the toilet roll holder? What will the future and technology have in store for us? Then what will be the big vise between man and women?

I remember while home from the navy for the weekend I would stay at my mom's house. She lived alone in her part of the house after I joined the navy and her tenant lived in the back apartment. What's nice about living alone is . . . Things are always just the way you leave them. There isn't anyone around to disturb your stuff or other things you touch on a daily basis; unless she too has experience the unexplainable happening from the vortex. So, anyway . . . I wake-up late at night and I go pee in the upstairs bathroom; you know fast and quick . . . don't look into the mirror . . . run for the safety of one's blanket. Well, later on that night I wake-up to the sound of, "AAAAhhhh!" The next morning, my mother kindly reminded me about putting the seat down. Seeing as I didn't live there anymore she didn't give it a second though about ensuring the seat is down. Perhaps she leaves the light off in the bathroom cause she doesn't want to look in the mirror either.

We both experienced a strange happening one night. I thought I heard something down stairs so I walked out of my bedroom and stood at the top of the stairs. I saw somebody with a ball cap and short jacket standing at the foot of the stairs. Before I could say anything he turned around the corner of the entry way, out of sight, towards the front door. As I was about to walk down the stairs to see what was going on . . . my mother came around from the other room, stood at the base of the stairs and asked what I was doing roaming through the house at night. I ran down the stairs and check the front door. It was locked, the dead bolt was latched, and I could see through the window of the door that the screen door was hooked from the inside. Hmmm. This was after my dad died and before I joined the navy. I never liked the front entryway and there was a closet there I dis-liked even more . . . I checked the closet as well!

So . . . which is worse . . . ? Not replacing the toilet paper onto the holder or forgetting that special someone's' birthday?

Outta Sbzzz Mind   by Sb Waitt

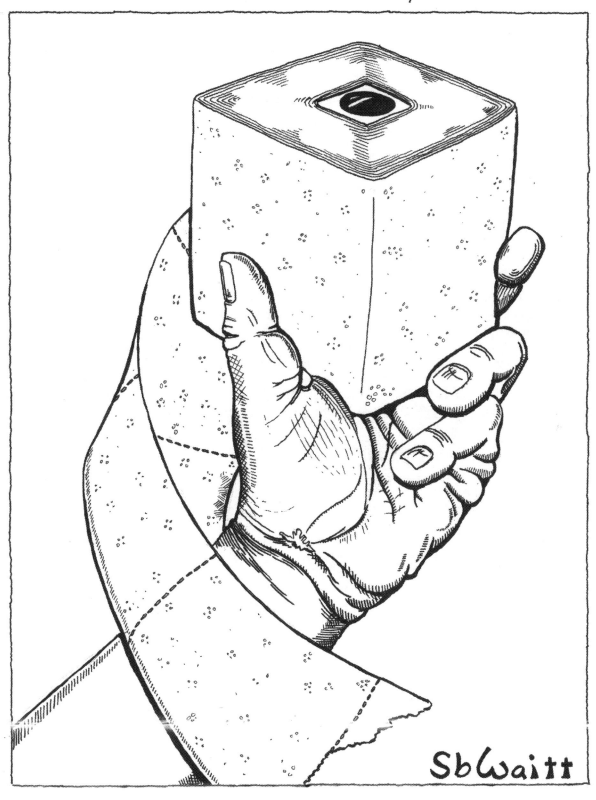

Mans greatest invention, a square roll of toilet paper

A SKULL FROM THE PAST

THE INTERNET CAN BE A wonderful thing. I made contact, with a fellow draftsman from my High School years. Dave W is his name and one of the first things he asked was, "Do you still draw pictures of skulls?" I didn't reply to his question right away. I smiled and the gears in my brain started to turn. I left the computer and walked to my drawing room, grabbed some paper and a pencil, and sketched a couple of ideas onto the paper. A few hours later I finished this drawing. All my drawings of skulls in school were drawn on the lined loose leaf notebook paper for note taking. My notes always had a doodle or two in with them. Well, it was more like I had a couple of notes attached to my doodles.

Dave and I graduated from Briscoe Junior High School and we were the two that were selected to attend Claude H Pattern Vocational High School for drafting. Our sophomore drafting class had two other graduates from the other Junior High School, Memorial. We were the four selected to attend the drafting class out of all the other candidates. I'd like to say we were the ones pick out from a batch of one hundred possible applicants . . . The truth is I don't have a clue how many other students applied to attend the drafting class. So I was one of the four in the classroom staring at each other. We stared our three year journey to learn how to properly push pencils and we all graduated together with the rest of Trade School and the High School. "Pencil Pushers" was the alternate name for draftsmen; this is before computers and the drafting program called Auto-CAD, if you're wondering. I thought you might be . . . All three of my drafting partners were named David. I was the only non Dave. I always thought I could be an honorary Dave for the day.

So I use to draw skulls from time to time. It was usually during the alternate week when we took our other required studies that was required in order for us to obtain a High School diploma along with our Trade School diploma. So I used to draw these skulls . . . I'd be asked by the other classmates, "Can you draw me a skull?" Course they would want this in it or that in it. Then they'd ask, "Can ya draw the skull like this, like that, or how ever way. Anyway, I would and did for the three years I went to school . . . I don't know what happened to all my sketches from back then? I'd like to ride a time machine to retrieve the ones I drew for myself.

During our drafting week of class one of my class mates that was a year ahead of me, I believed we called him Stieny or something like that; he'd draw ray guns . . . they were awesome. They were kind of the style you'd see in a Marvel Comic book. Well I couldn't resist, so I drew one with my ruler, compass, and triangle . . . It came out pretty good. Tim S. saw what I was doing and he walks over to my desk, picks up my drawing, and presented it to Stieny and said, "You have competition!" Stieny looks at my drawing and replied, "Yea, but I draw mine free hand."

I seldom use a straight edge, compass, or template when I drew for fun or drew anything that wasn't technical back then. In my mind a real artist could draw pictures without anything other than eye hand coordination. I didn't accept that rulers, compasses, templates and such were tools, aids, instrument that artists used to create their art. I use to practice for hours drawing circles and circles and circles wondering when I'd be able to perfect drawing a perfect circle. I'd do the same for ovals and straight line.

While aboard USS Harry E. Yarnell CG-17 In Norfolk Virginia from 1982 to 1984, I participated in a fun drawing class for 8 weeks at Old Dominion. My instructor and I use to due battle over techniques finally she said, "Hold the pen any damn way you want too." She had lots of patience with me. She also convinced me that it was ok to use rulers, compasses, templates and other devices when I draw . . . She said, "Sb, they are tools! Stop wasting time drawing and redrawing your circles!" I wish she added light tables to the list of tools back then. I didn't accept light tables until 1995 when I met an artist by the name of Donna E. She'd tell me, "It's OK to trace your own work! It's not ok to trace someone else's work and claim it as your own." I'm good at complicating things. Isn't that right Howard?

When I draw today, I like a little bit of crudeness in my drawings. I stopped the attempting of being a perfectionist. Then all of a sudden drawing wasn't a chore. I believed everyone would judge me because it wasn't pristine, perfect, or it wasn't the way I thought others would want me to draw. In my sketches I now use a template. When I finalize my drawing, I like to freehand it. I may trace my work, however it is freehand. The borders of my drawing I pencil with a straight edge and I ink it freehand. I like the non-perfect edges of my drawings.

I like the expression, "I am perfect in my imperfection." Now I may be miss quoting this next one, here goes . . . "To err is human to become perfect is insane or to be crucified."

Outta Sbzzz Mind by Sb Waitt

A skull from the past

HIGH HEEL ROLLER

ALRIGHT ALL YOU ACTION LOVERS . . . It's time to roll into action. A high heel roller is a real go getter in life, there's no holding you back. You set your sights for something and you go get it!. You're unstoppable! Regardless of work or play, "YOU-WILL-GO-ALL-THE-WAYYYYY!

I like this drawing. It is pretty clean as my drawings go. I thought it would make a great coffee mug and as well it will look good on someone's, "I love me wall." Do you have an, "I Love Me Wall?" That's a wall in your home where you hang up stuff about yourself, in'n ya didn't know? Paige liked this drawing. She uses it as one of her avatars from time to time on her computer. She's a high octane person!

This idea might make an interesting competitive event for the Summer Olympics when held in San Francisco. Can ya see yourself whizzing down the steep hills at breakneck speeds? Leaning low into the curves, fighting off your opponents for front position? You'll be giving it all you got, with . . . Agility, balance, stamina, and endurance!!! The streets will be lined up with enthusiastic cheering crowds, "The first one to reach the piers alive wins!" At the end of the line you be exhilarated by the taste, smell, and feel of victory! Cameras will be snapping off pictures of your smiling face.

Now I've walked the streets of San Francisco a few times over the years. It's pretty hilly and at times hard on the knees, legs, and feet if you're not in shape. It's a great place for training before entering a marathon. There is one stretch of this one particular street that has to be the steepest street in the country. I believe the street is named, Filbert Street.

In San Diego a section of Laurel Street is very steep. This section of road is not friendly to city buses or long vehicles. Traffic other than cars usually detours around this section of street. From time to time, a driver of a long vehicle doesn't pay attention where he is going. The bus, truck or other motor vehicle bottoms out, and becomes stuck and blocks traffic until a tow truck can winch it free. I'm sure there are other locations around our country where drivers put themselves in the same predicament.

I'm totally amazed how women can walk in heels all day long. Now add an incline such as a ramp or small hill and I'm totally baffled; especially walking down hill! They must have great balance, strong ankles and legs from wearing them every day if they chose too.

Back in the middle ages through the pre-colonial day's men would wear shoes with heels, shirt with ruffles, and wear wigs. I believe today they are called, cross-dresses. I saw a pair of shoes in the ladies section that I used to own and wear back in the early to middle 1960's; they were brown and white with an inch or so in height heel . . . In the past dating back to the time of the early Egyptians around 3500 BC some of the upper-class wore an elevated foot wear while the lower class walked barefoot or in sandals. Heels for men come and go, they seem like they will forever be attached to women.

I noticed there is an awareness charity called, "Walk a mile in her shoes." This is where men walk a mile in high heels to support the prevention of abuse towards women. Something to think about if you'd like to have another perceptive in life.

So again I say, If we could all walk a mile in someone else's shoes and experience what it is like to be the other person for a change; perhaps we would have a better world to live in. I believe we are here to be supportive of one another not knock one another down cause your board, greedy, of think it's amusing to pick on people. Why is there abuse in the world? Why, why, why. In this day and age I'd have thought we would have learned by now.

"The answer my friend is blowing in the wind, the answer is blowing in the wind." When ever I hear that song I get all misty eyed and think what it will take to get every one on the bandwagon of world peace. It starts with self. I've learned, you not able to give what you don't have. So we each have to find peace within before we spread it around to everyone.

I've thought of a day when all radio stations play the same songs at the same time for 24 hours. "A day of world peace," imagine the whole world listening and singing to songs such as: We Shall Over Come, Imagine, Peace train, What's Up, Bridge Over Troubled Water, Feed the Birds, Maybe There's a World, All You Need is Love, I'll Melt with You, You've got a Friend, I'd Like to Teach the World to Sing, and the list goes on and on. On the hour every hour it would be especially wonderful if the DJ's encouraged everyone listening to sing in unison. Imagine putting all that positive energy out to the world at one time. I would love to be a bird flying high in the sky listening to the world singing as one.

Can it be that simple? Why not! I say it is that simple. Repeat after me, "Today, I chose to do my part in ending abuse!" Then do it for: greed, war, harassment, self centeredness, murder, etc . . . It's that simple, we make simple things difficult when it doesn't have to be. Yep, "We shall live in peace."

Outta Sbzzz Mind by Sb Waitt

High Heel Roller

"MY LEFT HAND
IS A MONKEY HAND, AAAAAH!"

THIS DRAWING IS THE FIRST attempt of another drawing titled, "I've got voices in my head, Make'em stop!" I still like the drawing even though it didn't come out the way I wanted it too. So this is why he is screaming, "My left hand is a monkey hand, aaaaah!" When I finished the drawing what came to mind was. That hand looks like a monkey hand. Yep that's what I said. Do you agree that it looks like a monkey hand, kind of, sort of, maybe? Yes? No?

When I make fun of myself I like to include some realism. So my teeth are not perfect and when drawing my left hand you'll usually see a scare like design on my left wrist. The wrist scare is not in this picture, however. You might notice it in other drawings.

I wasn't very athletic as a teen or ever as that goes. Gym was never my favorite class. When participating in sports during gym. The chosen captains by the Gym Teacher would pick sides. I was always last to be picked . . . and when I was picked the eyes would roll and the comments would fly, "Not him, we already lost," or "go play with the girls!" They'd pick the guy with a broken arm, gimpy leg, or someone in a body cast before I was selected for a team. I have to admit I wasn't very good in team sports back then. I was always good for making at least two or three dumb plays like: I'd be open and alone in football someone would pass me the ball and I'd duck and let the ball fly over my head or hit a homerun ball and stay at second base . . . The list goes on and yes; today, I would go play with the girls if I could . . . Something wrong with a guy surround by ten girls???

So, when I was in gym class over at the High School side. We were required to take showers before leaving to our next class. There was this window open and a cool breeze was flowing in. The window was the push, pull, swivel kind. It was the only open window and it was located above my head out of arms reach by the clothes locker I was using. So I had the brilliant idea that I could jump-up and push the window shut. Yep, that's what I thought. What I didn't know was that the widow was stuck hard in this open position. So when I jumped up to push the window with my open palmed-hand, it kept going. It slid off the aluminum frame and went through the glass pain. The glass shards tore my wrist as gravity took over and I dropped downward to the locker-room floor. Ok, so my intelligent level was low and this is more proof to my agility and athletic ability.

So, I'm standing there with blood coming out of my wrist, I grabs the wrist, places my thumb over the cut, and I walks/runs to the gym office. A couple of the gym teachers are standing, talking, and joking as I enter. Finally, one of the teachers looks at me and says, "What do you want?" I held my arm out while covering the wrist and said, "I cut my wrist!" One of the teachers panicked a bit, because. He was sort of involved with the accident of a student a year or so earlier and never fully recovered from it even though it wasn't his (the Gym Teacher) fault.

A teacher drove me to the hospital. I don't remember anything between the times of going to the hospital up to the time the doctor was applying the stitches. I don't remember if I was told what a dumb or stupid thing you did? I do remember the doctor saying, "You were lucky! If it was a fraction of an inch over, you would have cut your artery."

Today if that would have happened and I was told that I'm lucky, I'd say, "I don't believe in luck." I might say I was fortunate. Luck doesn't involve reasons and circumstances. Luck is a way of denying personal power. Even by chance has a mathematical formula behind it. To me luck is winning the lotto and I didn't even buy the ticket. When I passed a test in school, I passed because I read the material and studied. Now if I filled in the scan-tron answer sheet without reading the questions and passed the test, which might be considered luck if there was a Leprechaun sitting on my shoulder.

Perhaps if I really did have a monkey hand back during the days of gym class, I might have been picked for a team before those with a broken arm? Monkeys are very good at jumping, climbing, running . . . I'd say they are athletic.

Outta Sbzzz Mind by Sb Waitt

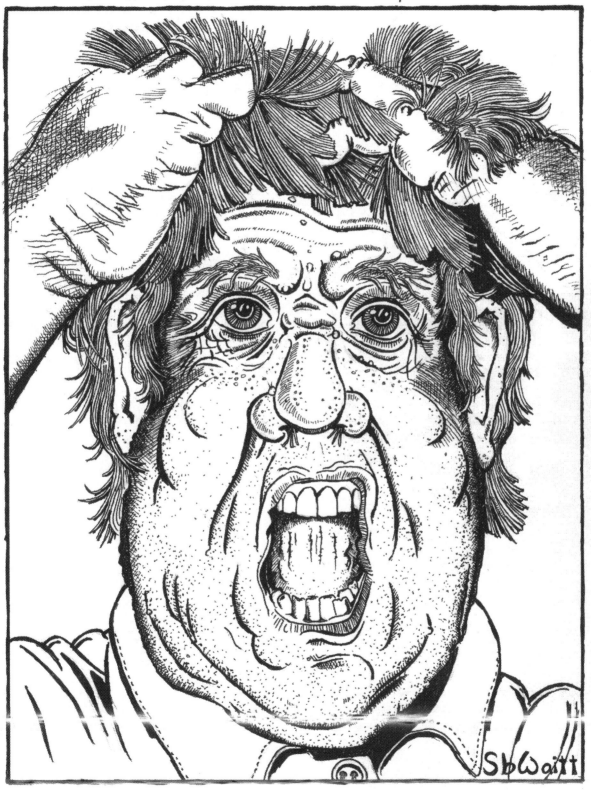

"My left hand is a monkey hand, aaaaah!"

IF I WAS SUPERMAN, I'D INCLUDE A POCKET PROTECTOR AS PART OF MY CLEAVER DISGUISE . . . THEN NO ONE WOULD KNOW MY SECRET IDENTITY . . . MAYBE I'D EVEN WEAR A PAIR OF RED SNEAKERS.

LOOK! UP IN THE SKY! It's a bird, it's a plane . . . Nope! It's Sb . . . Perhaps we've all seen the skits on TV how dumb Lois Lane and the rest of the people working for daily planet are. They are blind towards recognizing that the face of Superman with that curl of hair that drops down while in costume and Clark Kent hiding behind his glasses are one in the same. Yep, what a disguise! Genius, brilliant, "aaaaant (buzzer sound)" Not! I think one of the personalities could have given this disguise thing a little more thought . . . A bag would have been cleverer than Glasses or a curl of hair . . .

Now that I think about it his real name is Jor-El . . . So Jor-El has two disguises, Clark Kent and Superman . . . I'm a slow thinker, as well as a very slow and poor typist. Reporting would never be my first chose for work if I had to type and was paid by the hour. Not to mention that spelling thing . . .

If I was superman I'd . . . . Hmmm what would I do? What would you do? The choices are for greed, the betterment of the world, mess-up this world, destroy this world, or leave this world. I choose betterment of the world. Can ya think of any other possibilities?

We all have the freedom of choice. Well, unfortunately not everyone in the world has the freedom to exercise their choice without server repercussions. So what can we do about it? What can we create today, tomorrow, or next week to make this world a better place? There's a song called, "Better man," from the album, "Playing for Change: Songs around the World. The song has to do with self-improvement and it mentions making a better this world a better place. We do have to start with self because it is hard to give away that which we do not own. So let's say we all care about self and really mean it. Once you, me, I come first we can touch, move, and inspire the whole world to join in. It's your turn to come up with a possible solution.

There's and old navy saying, "If your not part of the solution your part of the problem." Now I know there are people that battle everyday to stay alive, feed their family, or are incapable of contributing to world problems right now. When you fight to keep you and your family alive, feed, and protected, you are doing your part to improve the world; the children are always our future. And one can never remind others enough about this point. Maybe one day they will turn it around, by themselves or with help. So what can we do, today so no one lives in a survival mode every day.

I believe the supermen and superwomen are those who give of self, make sacrifices, and do for others to support in the betterment of their family, home, committee, environment, the world, or some worthy cause. I have one charity that I have participated in since the year 2000. The name of the charity is, Big Animals for Little Kids. We entertain special needs children through dressing in animal costumes. The children love to hug these animals and the person in costume hugs back. We also do face painting and photograph the children with and animal of there liking and turn it into a button that they can wear as a memory of a warm fuzzy occasion!

I also support the USO with making soup and sandwiches on Fridays for the troops and their families. I do this with Mary and Mary Ellen we are part of what we call ourselves, "The Heart Team," out of love to support those in uniform and their family. You may not agree or believe in a military, however you have that right and they defend you and your rights regardless of your belief. It's kind of a paradox when you think about it. I/they defended your right to not agree, like, or want what I did for you.

I pray for a day when we will no longer need a military, a USO, a police department, FBI, jails, prisons, or a charity that brightens the lives of special needs children. Hmmm, "Imagine!"

All you super moms and dads and super non-parents out there . . . Good job; thank you for all that you do. All of the children are our future. They are our potential super men and women of today and tomorrow. There is a hero out there and if you look hard you'll realize it is inside of all of you. Hey, I remember this from a song . . .

So, if I was the supermen from the comic book could I make a difference in the world, yes. Could I turn around the negativity in the world in such a way that I would not be needed and I could hang up my cape; hopefully I can. Will I be able to unite the world into unity, peace, and end hunger? Will I touch, move, and inspire others to keep the changes which benefit all people? May the colors of my costume mean: Red (the blood of friendship,) White (world peace,) and blue (a clean and healthy environment.)

Outta Sbzzz Mind   by Sb Waitt

If I was Superman, I'd include a pocket protector as part of my cleaver disguise . . .
Then no one would know my secret Identity; Maybe, I'd even wear a pair of red sneakers too!

"I DON'T NEED ANYBODY TO EXPLAIN TO ME HOW TO CUT A CRUMMY PIECE-O-PAPER WITH A PAPER CUTTER!"

I'VE ENROLLED INTO COMMUNITY COLLEGE to take some art classes from time to time for fun. I always enjoyed listening to the instructions from the instructor regardless of the topic. I have a distorted outlook and like to twist things around. The outline given to us paints pictures in my mind of what to do, what not to do, and how to get on the wrong side of the art master. I like to live on the edge now and again; except when I feel like I'm hanging on for dear life.

There is always someone in the class that rebels and doesn't want to do anything the way the teacher says too, because they know more than anyone else in the class, or so it seems. We all have to battle applying the torturous techniques the art instructor wants us to learn. Eventually, when we are done with our studies, we create our art however we want to draw. We will continue to develop and enhance our own style or lack thereof over the years to come.

I had a friend that use to say, "You're crazy, everyone is crazy, the whole world is crazy, except me!" I enjoyed his outlook and his belief in him-self. He'd talk in this deep distorted Bostonian accent and do things his own way. Some things he was very successful at and others he was less than; yet, he'd keep plugging away in his world. I always got a chuckle from him. He was intelligent, only he didn't always apply his intelligence in a smart way.

So I like to twist and distort my face in a mirror. I enjoy drawing my face on paper and redraw again and again; until I've draw the twisted reality into a distortion that I like. When I look at this picture I can hear him screaming loud, "Ahh aaahhh owwwwww!" Yep . . . He knows the proper way to slice paper with the sharp handy-dandy paper cutter alright.

Sometimes, I only listen to myself and when I do . . . I usually get myself into trouble. I can hear Rocky J Squirrel saying, "And now, here's Mister Know-it-all!" What a way to live. Life is so much easier when I give up pretending to know everything and listen to others. We all have so much to share and add to life. It's OK to say, I don't know!" "I don't understand?" or, "Excuse me, my mind wandered off, I wasn't listening would you please repeat what you said again?"

Be thankful this" know-it-all attitude" is in the mind of an artist that you have no dependency on. It could be the surgeon that is about to perform brain surgery, "I don't need anybody to show me how to cut open a skull and perform brain surgery!" yep; the results will be brain salad surgery. Hmmm, how about your airplane pilot flying the plane you're riding in? What if you could hear the conversations going on behind the cabin door and you heard, "My co-pilot is crazy he doesn't know the first thing about flying a plane . . . Hey I wonder what this button does. It can't be important! Ahhh lets press it and see what happens." Whose flying the plane and why?

So think about that the next time you're on a plane, you hear the "ding" sound and the "fasten your seat belt" light is illuminated while the captain tells everyone to return to your respective seat. You might ask, "Why do we have to return to our seat now?" Hmmm, you will wonder if the captain, giving his spiel about why you must return to your seat, is true. You might find yourself reaching for the emergency information sheet tucked away in the pouch in front of you. Perhaps next time you'll pay attention to the flight attendant just before take-off.

If all this happens and the oxygen masks drop down as well; you might be in trouble specially if ya look out the window and he plane is still taxing down the runway before it ever lifts up off the ground. Sit back and enjoy your flight. If you have a question just press the "Attendant" button located right above your seat. Someone will be by shortly to attend to you every need . . . Hey how come the flight attendants are making a mass exodus down the runway?

If you ever take an art class and have a classmate that knows everything sitting next to you. You may consider taking a first aid class to supplement the art class. Stopping the bleeding and treating for shock is important and it may come in handy when "Mister Know-it-all" starts cutting paper unassisted. "Ahhh, I don't need your help!"

Outta Sbzzz Mind   by Sb Waitt

"I don't need anybody to explain how to cut a crummy piece-o-paper with a paper cutter!"

WAS, IS THIS THE PROOF
OF MY EXISTENCE?

WHEN I DRIVE OR WALK by cemeteries I wonder how people are remembered. Is there anyone that is alive who remembers or knows of them? As I grow older I think about what do I have to pass down to future generations. What and how will I be remembered? Will anyone care when I'm gone? I don't have any concerns if anyone will visit my grave because I don't want a grave . . . Sometimes I wonder does anyone care if I'm alive today.

Maybe that's why I putting together this book, legacy. I've collected a couple dozen songs and placed them on a Cd that I call legacy. I play it from time to time and think about what I will pass on before I die. I tell my children not to waste money in the funeral system. I want to go out the cheapest way possible. So if cremation is the cheapest way out, great. No casket, they use up valuable space. The world is getting crowded and cemeteries may be a historical item only in the future. Perhaps if you may, scatter a few ashes here and there around the world a bit for me. Burial at sea is an option if the Navy will perform the ceremony at no cost. I believe flowers are for the living, so send me flowers now not when I no longer walk upon this planet called earth. Ok, if I live on a boat for the rest of my days you can send me flowers to my boat. Each day it looks less likely that I'll ever make it to the moon, so the moon is out for sending flowers to me there! "Oh the pain, the pain!" to quote a memorable line quite often heard on a TV show called, Lost in space. Returning to the thought when I die . . . I want a happy memorial service with music that is, light hearted, fun and playful, children's music . . . I have a Cd with about 15 selections I'd like to be remembered by. The being remembered part is optional, though it might be nice.

So what's your proof of existence or is it not important to think about at this time? Will it be the grave stone only, or a grave marker? Maybe someone will plant a tree in your honor or dedicate a building, bridge or something else in your name? I wonder if my cat will miss me? It was explained to me that one of the differences between a dog and a cat is . . . When the owners dies the dog morns the loss and the cat goes out and looks for a new person to feed him or her. Another thing is when you feed a dog; he thinks, 'Wow! You must be God!' and when you feed a cat; she thinks, 'Wow! I must be God!

Now if I come back as a zombie you're probably not thinking about anything except survival! So cemeteries are officially out of business. Invest your money in home cremation units. Some cultures, around the world, bury their dead before sundown. You'll want to cremate the body before the temperature drops a few degrees. I wonder how much space is used in conventional cemeteries world wide.

Now, if you come back as a zombie, which type do you want to be, the fast kind or the slow type? When you make your decision are you thinking about your friends and family or are ya thinking bout those you don't care about? Do you want company or do you want to roam the earth alone?

Do you ever wonder if there is a here after, will there be dogs, cats, and animals, plants, swimming pools, carne asada burritos, cappuccino machines and chocolate brownies made the way my friend Gail P. makes them (Oh heaven on earth,) oh yea perhaps the bees won't have the need to sting? May all our allergies be cured?

Here's some songs I play when I think about legacy: "100 years," by Five for Fighting; "Dust in the Wind," by Kansas; "I Don't Want to Wait," by Paula Cole; "In My Life," The Beatles; "Live Like You are Dying," by Tim McGraw; and "One Kind of Favor," by Peter, Paul, and Mary

Do you ever go to the cemetery? I think they are spookier today than they were when I was a young child; back then, at night, I would slowly walk in looking for spooks, spirits, ghosts and goblins. Today, I'm pretty sure I don't want to meet any; however, I may not have any choice. I find the old cemeteries that don't have perpetual care are the more interesting ones to visit. The stones tilt, some have crumbled, moss growing on the side, or they have splintered.

The last time a bunch of us explored a grave site we'd look for familiar names; burry ourselves in the leaves in front of a grave stone and stretch an arm out of the pile while someone took the picture. I never did any stone rubbing even though there were a few that would look good on a wall in a frame. It's funny when you find a grave with a friends name on it, snap a picture, and when you present the picture to the respective friend . . . They don't want to look at the picture.

I'm curious, do you know of any cemeteries that play music and are automated? It could be a deterrent for vandalism. Imagine, at night, walking into a garden of the dead and creepy music starts to play, eerie sounds flow through the air, things pop-up out of open graves, smoke billows from the ground, ghost like apparitions appear, a hoot owl some trees, statues with luminous eyes, and a scream and a flash of light from the old mausoleum. I'd enjoy watching the surveillance footage . . .

Outta Sbzzz Mind   by Sb Waitt

"I HATE SHAVING!"

SHAVING IS NOT ONE OF my favorite things to do to pass the time away. When I first started to have facial hair appear I use to tell people I was going to pluck the hairs out so I wouldn't have to shave. My dad had other ideas. He'd make me shave when I didn't want to. I'm not sure when I started to shave on a regular basis before joining the navy or afterwards. In the navy, shaving is a daily task.

My boot camp company commander said, "You will shave every morning whether you have whiskers on your face or not . . . And I don't want to see any peach fuzz on your face for morning inspection, either!" So, everyone shaved in the morning regardless of how smooth their face felt. There were a few times where we'd be made to dry shave if the face wasn't free of hair or peach fuzz. The Company Commander would get right in your face to inspect, you'd feel the air exhaling out of his nose.

Being in Navy Boot-camp was an interesting experience during the summer months of 1976. Not everything back then had to be politically or humanisticaly correct. I wonder what it's like today. Seems like as time goes on there have been changes with what is acceptable and what isn't acceptable to get the point across to the new recruits. There is so little time to do so much and learn how to live with others as a team. Your life is dependant on your buddy or fellow shipmate as is their life with you.

On my first deployment I summated a request chit to grow a beard. My first class petty officer in charged asked me, "Can you grow a beard?" I said, "I don't know?" He looks at me, smiles, and says, "I'll approve it and pass it up the chain of command." I found out shortly after the started to grow that I hated the moustache. It never filled in with my facial hair . . . or, should I say the lack of. Eventual I shaved of the lip hairs and kept the rest . . . As long as I kept it trimmed, short, and clean around the edges I was allowed to keep it.

The beard to me meant less cutting of the face . . . I believe it was January of 1986 when beards were no longer allowed in the navy with the exception of medical reasons.

The big thing about shaving in the military is to shave about an hour prior to a dress white inspection. Attempting to stop the bleeding is dangerous while in one's white uniform. Blood on the collar is like a light house beacon in the night. As the expression or cliché' goes, "It stands out like a sore thumb!" It's kind of funny standing for inspection with little wards of paper stuck to the face. The inspector might say something like, "Did those little wads of paper on your face come with your sea bag that was issued to you in Boot camp?" You'd reply, "No sir!" He'd turn his head towards the man recording his comments and say, "Make a note that this man failed." You're in the hands and sense of humor of the inspector who determine your outcome of passing or failing. If you fail, coming in on a Saturday morning for a re-inspection it's so enjoyable . . . Not really! Liberty and off time is so precious.

I'm at the point now I only shave about once sometimes twice a week, no one to inspect me. I do annually grow a beard around the winter holiday season. I play Santa from time to time and I find the fake beard works better over a light base of real hair.

I've owned and used a couple electric razors over the years my last one got lost in the move from Cherry Valley to San Diego. Maybe some one will invent a pill to replace shaving, "time to take your shaving pill." I'd like the idea of a face cream to the face to remove the whiskers and facial hair, except the image of my face burning off come to mind. Chemical burns are not nice to receive. Plus we dump enough chemicals down the drain that end up in our water as it is. What can and cannot be filtered and removed to protect the environment is the question and thought to hold in any future or current invention.

Sometimes when I shave I'd swear I'm taking the skin and fresh right off the bone. Course we men only deal with the face and neck usually. Women shave their legs and armpits which is more surface area and more chances of nicks and cuts. Now wrestlers, body builders, and serious competition swimmers shave their entire body, almost; no thank you, not for me. Course with my physique, you wouldn't want to see my upper body. I'm doing everybody a favor.

I find it hard to imagine allowing a barber to shave ones face with a straight edge razor. It looks like something out of a horror movie. In movies we see old time explorers out in the wilderness breaking out their hunting knife giving themselves a close shave. Ouch . . . I wonder if chiefs every shave themselves with a sharp carving knife. Think about that the next time you go out to a fancy or family style restaurant. Yep I shave as little as possible today. I don't like to go to long cause then I have to do some pre-cutting with the scissors. Maybe before Thanksgiving I'll grow a beard and do a pre-cut with the electric carving knife and then I'll use a sharp—hand knife to shave with just for the experience.

Outta Sbzzz Mind   by Sb Waitt

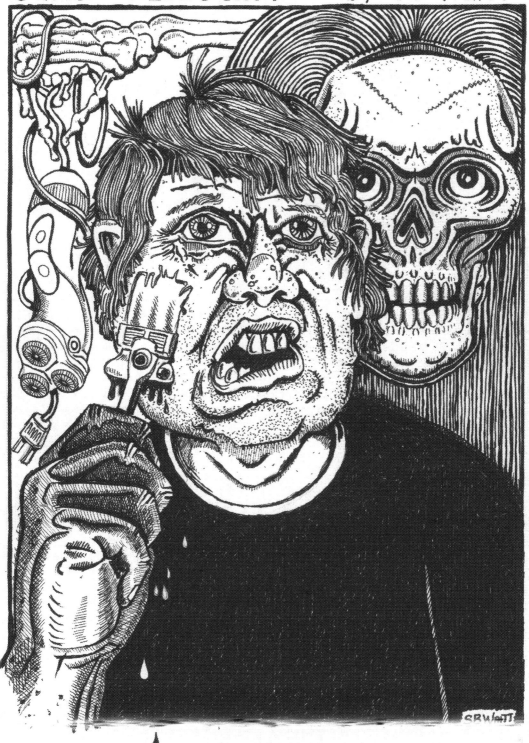

"I hate shaving!"

CARROT MONSTER I

"The Great Vegetable Rebellion"
Lost in Space
The way I would have created the monster in the episode!

THIS WAS MY FIRST ATTEMPT at recreating the Carrot Monster from Lost in Space. I was happy with it for a while. I even made a copy of it and sent it off to a sci-fi magazine thinking they would like it so much they'd put in the next issue. I went into fantasy land as if this cartoon would inspire TV networks to do battle with one another for which station would recreate the show. Yep, fame and fortune, 'Lost and space' is back on the air. All from this (in my mind) incredible drawing . . . Several weeks later I received one of those polite rejection letters stating something to the effect of, "We have our own artist and are not looking for any new people to join the staff at this time." I put the drawing, which I had ready to send off in the mail at a moment's notice, into my drawer with the other drawings and went on to something else.

My favorite TV show as a child was and is still 'Lost in Space.' It started out as a serious show and then developed into a comedy most of the time. However, it was always entertaining to me, regardless of the subject matter or the way the show was presented. I'd always relive the episodes over and over and add a little more seriousness to the episode. Yep, for years after it went off of primetime, I still thirsted for more. I am and will forever be "Lost in Space!"

In this one particular 3rd season episode, titled "The Great Vegetable Rebellion," Dr. Smith takes the space Pod down to a planet, that the Jupiter II and family is orbiting, while a birthday party celebration is going on. Smith's intentions were to bring back real flowers as a present for motives not so admirable. He becomes captured, on this world where vegetation is the highest form of life and he is forced to undergo a metamorphic transformation (this sounds good the special effects aren't so special.) Once the Robinson family, Major Don West and the Robot land on this planet covered with vegetation. They begin the search for Smith . . . Anyway there is this giant carrot (its giant for a carrot not for a person in costume) figure named Tybo and he is in charge of everything in this area of the planet. He wants to turn every one of the Jupiter II's crew into a plant of some kind! One of the best lines the carrot has is, "Moisture, I need moisture!" and then you'd see him lumbering towards a gas pump type of machine and he'd spray himself down with water. Dr. Smith uses the same line as well near the end of the episode.

This episode was determined to be the worst episode of the series run. I don't agree, I give my vote for the least desirable to watch is, "The Questing Beast." Bottom line with this show, it's my escape in life. It's where I go for safety, fun, and adventure! In my computer room I have pictures of the Robinson's hanging on my wall. I hum and whistle the theme song almost every day.

There were a several other episodes where the family encounters alien vegetation. One of my favorites is where these giant plants had duplicating powers. Judy was duplicated and fell into a state of suspended-animation/asleep in the giant pod. Her double infiltrated the Jupiter attempted to play like she was the original Judy, steal the fuel required for lift-off of the space ship, and use it for food for the plants . . . There is more to the story and I wanted a second part to it at a later time. Most of my favorite episodes were in the first season when they all lived in a black and white world. I'd say my favorite season was the first year and the next best was season three. If it came back on with new episodes I'd be recording it. Regardless of what anyone else says, it's my show.

I occasionally go into the internet searching for new and old stuff about the show. Sometimes I find and interview or blooper about the show. There are some sights where people will write stories and "Lost in Space" pops up once in a while. I found a new pilot show for the recreation of the series, it didn't sell. I want whatever comes out new to pick up or at least not nullify the original show. In sci-fi anything goes.

What's your favorite show from your youth? If you could only watch one show what would it be? The one you may later write stories too, even if you're the only one to read them. Perhaps you have sound tracks of music for the show. Do you own the DVD collection? Maybe there is a theme song or melody that you whistle, sing, or hum too aloud? Perhaps you've joined fan clubs and acquired pictures to reminisce by. Maybe you doodle something about the show in your school note book? For whatever your reason is: entertaining, touching, funny, serious, an escape, fantasy, or just because!!! That is good enough, because. It's your personal reason. Enjoy, I do because I am forever, 'Lost in Space!'

Outta Sbzzz Mind   by Sb Waitt

Carrot Monster I

CARROT MONSTER II

SO THIS IS MY LATEST and greatest recreation of the Carrot, from an episode of 'Lost in Space' as mentioned in the previous drawing. This monster would have been as big as the Cyclops monster in the first season and pilot episodes; maybe bigger! He is definitely meaner, faster, and dangerous. He's kind of like a T-Rex . . . Maybe a C-Rex: Carrontisaurus-Rex.

In my version of this particular episode "The Great Vegetable Rebellion" the space pod is being tested for maneuvers with a new retro-rocket that needed to be replaced; in the safety of orbit around an un-inhabited planet. They thought it was a good test spot without the fear of aliens attacking. There is tons of vegetation and oxygen detected on this planet, so this will also be an ideal spot to load up on needed supplies. After the pod's retro-rockets are tested and passed; the pod was to land and find a good location for the Jupiter II to land.

My version didn't have plants screaming from being cut with a machete blade! Yes, outside on the planet has oxygen rich air and that's the best part for the Robinsons and company. The vegetation is poisonous and some have animal characteristics, some even leave the ground and move around to hunt. The food they find that they believe is safe to eat has another twist to it!

This would be a good home world for the original black and white movie, "The Thing." Their cities have been dead for hundreds of years. No power sources that work anymore. Their technology went wild so those with space ships left. So of-course before the Jupiter II leaves this world they will encounter a thing or two! This story is still in its note and scribble stage.

I never liked the idea of being stranded on alien world for a whole season. You know, back in the days of when a season of shows total more than 26. What are we down to now, 20 episodes per year? However, a series of shows with a particular story line of 4-8 episodes or so worked for me before the Jupiter II would blastoff into space again. I like the idea of flying in space, landing on a world, not always monsters, not always guest stars, not always planets with a breathable environment . . . I really like the soap style of TV because good things that work can return . . . Especially in Sci-fi, there is always a way to bring back the dead regardless of how they were killed!

I have four journals with my lost in space stories, I've cleaned up two of the journals and put them into the computer. I've typed about a quarter into the third story. When I'm involved with my projects, the ideas flow. Now whether someone else likes them is another story? They are a starting place for other possibilities!

The more I read or draw, when I walk away and return from a break; I then see things differently. I want to make the changes for the better. Unfortunately, for me, this keeps going on and on. Yes, there is a perfectionist side of me. This comes from my years of a draftsmen and being in the navy. Perfectionist can have a habit of stopping me from accomplishing what I intended to create from the beginning. Why; because, the outcome at the present time is never good enough for me. Everything has to be perfect so, I'd rather not do it if it isn't gonna come out perfectly. The downside is my expression of art and writing is never seen by anyone. The ideas stay locked up in my head and are forever on the computer or in a draw for a later time when I can make things perfect stage. So I'm not keying on everything has to be perfect. I'm allowing my imperfections to be presented. I don't have to measure up to other people!

We all have good ideas and not everyone is going to like them; so what, how many millions of people are in the world? Some may say they like your ideas; however, they only then remind you of all the negative things and outcomes about your work. So we listen only to the negative comments about my, our, your work and it never comes in the public view. You see, you are competition to people that you have no idea that you're competition too! Amazing isn't it. You're better then you believe you are. You're wonderful, you're intelligent, you're likeable, you're creative, and you're magnificent! Regardless of being male or female, you are a High heel Roller and don't see it! So, do those things you like to do!

Outta Sbzzz Mind   by Sb Waitt

Carrot Monster II

"I'VE SEEN ENOUGH, GIVE ME THE KEYS!
I'M TAKING OVER"

I'M NOT VERY POLITICAL MINED. In fact I really didn't start voting until there was a motion on the ballet about approving the building of a baseball only stadium in the downtown San Diego Gas Lamp area. All the years I served in the navy, someone else chose who was going to be my Commander and Chief. That would be President Carter, Ragan, Bush, and Clinton. One would think all of us in the military would vote and have some say in who was going to be our overall boss.

As time creeps by, I keep telling myself that I will read the paper every day specially the political columns; well, I sometimes read the political cartoons, that's as far as I've ventured into the political world. I do own a Watergate coloring book. Most likely not many of you remember or care to know about the Watergate incident involving President Richard Nixon, Vice President Spiro Agnew and other members of his cabinet . . .

I have to admit I like to watch the show, "Tabitha Takes Over." I find her very attractive, alluring, and I like the way she conducts her business when consulting with the owners and staff of the hair salons. She has that, "don't mess with me I am the boss kind of attitude." My reaction out loud is usually, "woof, ahhh! I like it!" What's the expression, "I like the way she struts her stuff!" Bob Segar has a song, "Her Strut," that could be her running song . . . So strut away Tabitha, strut away!

I can see Tabitha authoritatively walking into the capitol building (she is positively strutting her stuff) and directly into the oval office or up on stage at one of the presidents weekly meetings where he address his business to the country, staff, or who ever. All becomes quiet and she steps up, walks over to the president, she engages his eyes, she puts her open hand out with the palm up, and says her line, "I've seen enough, hand me the keys. I'm taking over!"

I wonder what the Capitol building, interior and exterior will look like when she is finished with the redesign and make-over? Will the white house still be called the white house when she is finished with her changes? Perhaps, our flag will have some new innovative ideas like . . . Stars that twinkle, scrolling illumination of the strips, maybe an occasional bomb bursting in the air, like the fourth of July, will appear on the flag, and/or shoot out of the top of the staff! Will the capitol building be green to blend in with the lawn and trees? She may feel that there are way too many marble colored buildings in Washington and perhaps a change like this is a good thing!

We live in a grand and glorious free country that doesn't put us in prison because we don't agree with, satire and joke about, or humiliate the president. It's good to know that freedom of speech is present and alive in America. Freedom of speech also applies with pictures, drawings, cartoons, songs, movies and the list goes on and on. Of course, we did have a president that; I'm not sure if he knew how to read anything outside of the Sunday comics . . . Hey, come to think of it, neither do I. I do sometimes read the sports section and look at the computer ads, and save the coupons for the savings on groceries that's about it.

Long live The United Sates of America and all of us living under the drool, prose and rhetoric of those governing. I may kid however this is the country I want to live in. I believe it has the most to offer.

I served and would gladly serve again in the military so all can live they way they want to regardless of who ever doesn't agree or approve. I still remember the First Code of Conduct, "I am an American. I serve in the forces that guards our country and our way of life, I am prepared to give my life in your defense." I'd go back in the service tomorrow if the powers that be would authorize my re-joining. I really enjoyed the camaraderie, each day was different, the salt air while at sea aboard US Naval ships, and traveling to new places and ports for liberty call.

I wonder what it would be like aboard a ship with Tabitha in charge and at the helm. There are those words again flowing in through the ear and on into the brain. The words are now singing, dancing, and flowing through my mind till finally, "Captain, I've seen enough, hand me the keys. I'm taking over!" I believe she can place the fear of the clam into the hearts and minds of the crew! She'll start her speech to the crew assembled on the fantail, "The fun and games are over! You will get down to business. I run a taut ship and rule with an iron clad fist! Etc . . . etc . . . etc . . . blaa, blaa, blaa . . . The male crew will slowly become hypnotized and serve willingly under her command.

In all fairness this is the 21st century so the ladies, women and girls you're going to have to tell me who your dream captain would be. I have no idea these days. I do know many of the women like her in the beginning. When she comes back to visit at a later time; it seems like everybody is all kisses and hugs to her.

Outta Sbzzz Mind   by Sb Waitt

"I've seen enough, give me the keys! I'm taking over!"

51

WHAT I WANT
IS A NEW PAIR OF EYES

AS I AGE I FOUND my eyes are in a stage of regression. The first time I notice my eyes aren't what they use to be was in my rack in the navy aboard USS Leahy CG-16 reading a book. The word rack is another word for bunk or bed in civilian terms. The rack is like a big square pan with a nice 'comfortable' 3 inch thick mattress of the cheapest foam you can find. In rough weather I'd stick my shoes under the mattress so I wouldn't roll out and fall upon the deck (floor) when the ship would shake, roll and slam down hard into the sea because of the wind and waves. Anyway, I was reading a fine print book and realized my arms weren't almost long enough. I held the book as far away as I could and the words where no longer blurry. Today my arms would have to be longer than a baboons' arm, I use magnifiers of different strengths depending on whether I am drawing or reading.

The next time I had difficulties with seeing what I was doing was in an art class while at Mira Mesa College (course I didn't know it at the exact moment.). I was drawing a picture and had a difficult time drawing straight lines for this shading chart. It was to be freehand and the effect was to be created using straight lines only. Yes it is the same thing over and over, Mister Instructor wanted us to shade it one way only, we had to hold the pencil one way only, and they had to be sharpened one way only . . . I think before we are allowed to call ourselves artist we have to be tortured with all these screwy techniques and rules. Yes at times it is frustrating; however, we may have the same teacher for a semester or two or more before we are through. Then we move into a new class the particulars start all over again. This too shall pass.

Anyway, I was drawing or attempting to draw straight lines . . . One of my class mates noticed I was having a hard time and asked, "What is the matter with yoouuuu?" I said, "I'm having a hard time drawing straight lines." He said, "Here, give my magnifiers at try." Yep, that was it. All of a sudden I could see the lines and drew them straight and apart they way I wanted too (actual at the time . . . The way the instructor wanted me too.) Then the realization hit me, I needed glasses!

I got up out of my seat and walked outside, bought a soda from the machine, drank part of it before I returned to class. My instructor came over to me and said, "Hey it's not time for a break yet!" I said, "Yes it is!" I told him what happened and he said, "You only take breaks when I tell you too!"

So now I have lots of magnifiers of various strengths to use depending on what I'm doing. I use low magnification for the computer, stronger for reading and very strong for when I'm drawing. I think it's time to go back and have my eyes checked. A couple years ago I had my eyes checked. My doctor at the time said I wasn't ready for prescription glasses, yet. Perhaps, 'Yet' is here! No the lapse time since my last eye check-up . . . 6 years ago, yep it's 'yet!'

It's amazing what I don't see or realize till I put on a pair of magnifiers. I hate when I forget to grab my glasses when I go out to the store. I usually borrow a pair from the magnifier rack in the store and before I check-out I return them to their rightful spot. I think I'll make a sticker to place on the glasses I borrow that says, "Approved and tested by Sb."

I like to keep the magnifier glasses scattered around the house. The stronger ones I keep by my drawing table, the weakest I use for watching TV, ones that are stronger than the TV I use at the computer, and ones that are weaker than the drawing ones I use for reading. It's a system that works until a couple of pairs break. Then I'm back to, "Where's my glasses for . . ."

Sometimes when I go to the book store I grab the wrong ones. It's hard to browse when I'm wearing my drawing glasses and I have to be about a foot away from the shelf to see. It's like having tunnel vision and it gets old fast; however, I'm growing old slow. A piece of advice to all of you with good eyes, protect your eyes while you're young and you may not need glasses till you're much older. Use sunglasses in the bright sun, especially while driving.

As I hold this pair of eyes I know I wouldn't want to take a bit of it, yuck. The thought of chewing on one of those eye balls disgusts me. Being able to grow a new set of eyes from a fruit tree is a great idea. Perhaps we could grow other organs within the fruit such as a heart or kidney. Scientists would have to use a bigger fruit for the lungs and liver. Fruit and vegetables are not the same as animals; but, who knows what will happen with genetics. It seems like if we can think of an idea, someone will invent a way for it to happen. This will come in handy during long voyage space flights.

Let us not forget about a new pair of legs and feet, arms and hands, or a new pair of ears. This notion is impossible today, yes, maybe not tomorrow.

Outta Sbzzz Mind   by Sb Waitt

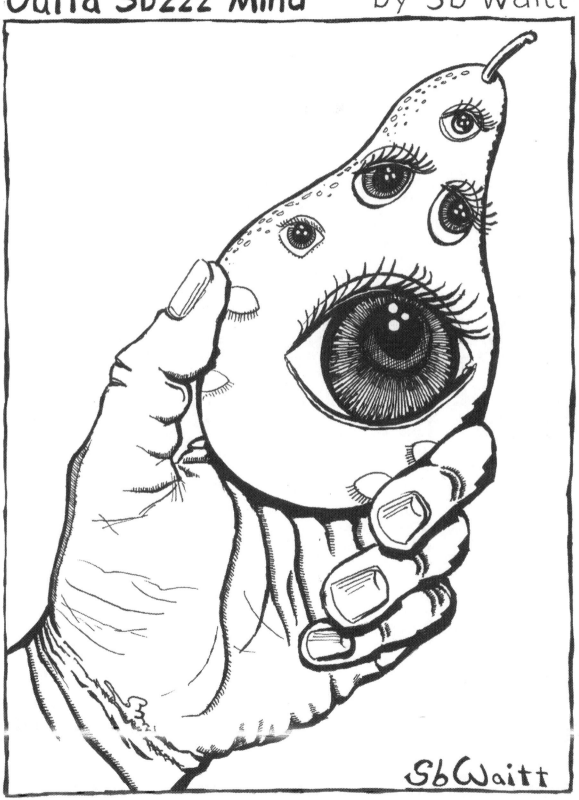

What I want is a new pair of eyes

MEANWHILE
AROUND THE RINGS OF SATURN

SO WHAT IF THERE WAS life around the planet Saturn. Would they be suspicious of aliens from earth stopping by one day to invade their home world? When earth space probes flew past their cameras and detectors, would they scream about UFO's or whatever their compliment is that means the same thing? If they probed the earth's skies would they discover our radio waves? Would they see the old reruns from our TV stations or hear all our radio transmissions? Would they want to watch them at all . . . Perhaps, after watching a few of our broadcasted TV shows they may determine that earth really has no intelligent life on it! Maybe they will enjoy the music? Isn't music a universal language or form of communication?

One day in space court, NASA might have to stand trial for all the junk they launched up there that is floating around in space. They might be sued for the debris that crashes into their atmosphere; destroying whatever the debris' lands on such as their homes, precious structures, and the occupants of the planet or moon (there are no rules that say only planets harbor life.). I thought when the space shuttle went into existence that they (NASA) might retrieve some of the old junk, parts, and broken satellites before returning the shuttle with crew to the ground. Maybe the next shuttle type vehicle that is built, commissioned, and launched into space on a regular routine, will perform the task of space clean-up?

I find it scary that on any given night or day we could be hit from whatever doesn't burn up in our atmosphere on re-entry. Imagine waking up to a unfamiliar sound and it turns out to be part of the space station has destroyed the car, is planted in the middle of your living room or a multitude of other possibilities. How much does space junk go for these days, is it profitable?

So the space probe is in orbit around one of Saturn's moons, for example. Their space camera energizes, focusses in on the orbiting satellite and transmits a video image back to earth, and then this happens. An alien (to us it's and alien to them we are the aliens) space craft pulls up to the satellite and locks onto it. An extraterrestrial climbs out of his ship and opens up a pad of some kind and starts to write sometime on to it. When he/she/it finishes what appears to be writing onto a pad of paper, he rips off a piece of it and affixes it onto the satellite . . . Once this act is performed our receiving units lose the signal and our screens go blank. For the next thirty days no more contact! The very next day (day 31) our receivers pick up a video stream again. This spaceship that looks like a tow truck pulls up and tows it away. So NASA would be charged with illegal parking, littering, and abandonment of a vehicle . . . Maybe they will have more charges than we can think of!

Another thought comes to mind . . . The space alien holds up a sign that reads, "Bring Back V!" or some other show that they liked to watch that was canceled. I'm still thinking a version of Lost in Space will come back and pick up where the show left off (have I mentioned this before? Ok, once or twice . . .) I don't believe they would want to see more of, 'My Mother the Car,' 'the green Hornet,' 'Soap,' or 'the evening Nightly News?' However, it's . . . their 'wants and opinions' that count for the return of whatever show they enjoy watching . . . not ours.

One other possibility is: a huge ship lands in Washington DC on the front lawn of the Capital building . . . The ship splits open and three quarters of it rises up on an angle, a metallic flap opens from the back, and all this old space junk slides out! You know? It's like a humongous space dump truck! The ship moves forward to ensure all the stuff slid out of the back, it closes up; it floats upward, and then hovers over the capital. From the ship, it sends out a voice transmission with a video picture of the dumping sequence that all see! Next, the audio cuts in and transmits a signal that everyone in the USA can hear. It over rides all signals on the radio, TV, and energizes all loud speaker systems and says, "Hey, Did You guys forget about this stuff," and then zooms off out of sight?

I'm all for the space program. I want more that what is happening. I look forward to new discoveries and new ideas coming into existent. As a child, I imagined a world like the old Jetsons TV show where we'd be flying around with jet packs and flying motorized vehicles that would slowly replace the gasoline automobile. I was disappointed when I realized the year 2000 was not going to be any big deal. Ok the biggest thing we have is computers and they are all neat and stuff; however, I wanted to be in space personally. I thought by 2001 we'd be experts at flying out to the planet mars and beginning to mine the asteroid belt between Mars and Jupiter. In my mind back then I envisioned NASA would be ready to take the leap and travel to Jupiter and Saturn.

Today, we are gearing up to return to the moon. I still wonder if a man and woman will step upon the planet Mars before I die. Will SETI make contact or an alien land publically here for all to see; I'd like to be here for both of those one too.

by Sb Waitt

Outta Sbzzz Mind

Meanwhile . . . Around the rings of Saturn

"THIS TIME YOU CLEAN UP THE MESS
IF THEY GET SICK!"

I'M SURE WHEN THE ALIENS pick up or abduct unsuspecting people the get space sick from time to time. Someone has to clean up the mess. Do ya think they enjoy that part of there job. I think not!

When I was a teenager I use to go walking at night with the belief that a flying saucer would fly over me and "beam me up!" It never happened, so years later as an adult I'd do the same thing; only now, I drive to my desired destination and watch the sky. Yep. It never has happened. Now I go out into my backyard and star gaze with the same dream. Every falling star or slow moving light teases my desire.

I enjoy following the planets through the night sky and occasionally I break out a pair of binoculars to search and look at things at a closer view. I'll enjoy staying outside for an entire lunar eclipse when it occurs. I watch for falling stars and imagine one landing in my backyard. The newspaper informs me when the various planets rise and set. My friends and neighbors where amazed that I knew where the planets were. Sometimes they'd look at me in disbelief. I'd reassure them where I received my information from, however. They would forget quickly.

I watch the science channels in search of new shows about space travel, our solar system, the universe, and UFO's. I re-watch the old shows over and over. they quenches the thrust for a short period. I even like to watch the show, "Meteor men."

I dream of being on an expedition for meteorites. I start digging and find something a little more than a meteorite. I want to find that buried spaceship that has been beneath the earth for a long time. I imagine, climbing inside and the ship comes to life and whisks me away to its home world. Sounds like a movie.

I find it hard to believe that we are the only form of life with intelligence. I would like to believe when we do make contact that the visitors will be friendly and not here to invade. Based on the history of our world I'm not to sure if they will be friendly. The men of old that have been sent out on a quest to explore our world seem to end up with some form of domination, overthrowing the weak, or not speaking the truth with the local natives. Not all explorers have been this way! The expeditions that I remember from history were and end up conquering for the homeland. Of course I am growing older and becoming a little more confused with each day.

Friendship is wonderful, nice, and civilized, yet greed appears to be a prime motivator to the strong, corrupt and unwise. Ever listen to the song "39" by queen? That song is one on my favorite songs about space explorers. This is a good people explorer song with nice aliens. Those are the ones I want to meet.

On dark nights I like to play the music of Lost in Space, especially the theme song from the third season. I imagine myself driving the chariot over rough terrain on an alien world. I can hear the Robot bellowing out, "Warning, Warning! Danger ahead!" I'll have to evade and escape from the 60 foot Cyclops that is hurling boulders at my all-terrain vehicle. Ahhh, what an exhilarating life.

It's fun to fantasize. My favorite place to drive and imagine I was on an alien world is Utah, the Grand Canyon, Zion National Park and Meteor Creator. Such an awesome view, creation in its glory . . . Great rock formations, amazing colors, all to stimulate the mind, my thoughts went wild. I always thought the colors were enhanced when I'd look at pictures of Zion Park, nope! The colors in the pictures are not as brilliant.

The thought of being abducted by aliens that want to cut the body my open to analysis and compare the different physiology between them and us scares me. Imagine being strapped to a table and a long needle is slowly being lowered towards you eye. I have nightmares about that thought, I hate needles. Being prodded and probed doesn't sound fun either. How about waking up momentarily, see your arm or leg has been severed, and laid out next to your full of wires, electrodes, and long flexible tubes connected to a devise that pumps synthesized blood to keep your body parts and you alive.

Lots of strange noise and lights, as the aliens talk in an unfamiliar language. You begin to scream only to find you're unable to; because, there is a devise around your neck suppressing the use of your vocal folds (vocal chords) in your Larynx. When they look at you, will you see an frightful and terrifying expression on their face or will it be expressionless, peaceful, or will they all be wearing a mask of some kind? Maybe they will expose you to various gases that will put you into a convulsion, force you to eat alien food, or put you in a room will all kinds of creepy crawler things that bit and sting? Perhaps you'll be immersed in a watery solution or gelatinous goo of some kind and you won't be able to hold your breath. What if you wake up and see your body and find you're in someone else's body? Maybe they will alter your skin in some way? You may find out what animal mutilation is all about whether you want to know or not.

Will you wake up in a safe place when it is over? Will you have nightmares with bits and pieces of a memory you want to forget? Perhaps your encounter was pleasant and you wait for another opportunity?

Outta Sbzzz Mind

by SbWaitt

SBWAITT

"This time, you clean up the mess if they get sick!"

THE FAMOUS ONE FOOT PIZZA

WHEN I WAS A CHILD this is what came to mind anytime I'd see on a menu, "one foot pizza," or from other eating establishments one foot this or one foot that. So of course I'd draw a picture of a waitress carrying out a pizza with a foot on it. I have a couple doodles of one foot food items that will make it into a future book. May you'll enjoy them all. I know I do. They may not be tasty. I find them humorous. May it not make you want to hurl and never go to a restaurant again? Restaurants are fun to go to and we don't have to wash the dishes afterwards unless you forget your wallet. You know I don't know of or remember any of my friends ever forgetting their wallet and are forced to wash dishes or the owner will call the police. I think it only happens in movies and TV shows.

As a child the tomato was one of my least favorite food items. Any time my parents took us out or brought home a pizza I'd eat the pizza with everything scraped off of it. Yup, the crust was all I wanted. I don't remember when I started liking tomato sauce. I'd eat spaghetti with butter no sauce in the early stage of my life, not now though, I want it all . . . sauce, bread, butter, meatballs, sausage! Back then I was a pretty picky eater as a kid. I didn't even like catsup either. I believe it was that hamburger quick food place where I started eating hamburgers with catsup and all the other stuff that was on it, because my dad didn't want to special order a hamburger for me without catsup. Those special orders would take forever without the pickles, chopped onion, catsup, and mustard. Plain burgers were so much better tasting in those days to me. I still enjoy a fresh burger off the grill plain to this day. The 'unadulterated Burger' in-between a soft or toasted bun I call it.

Being from New England tarter sauce was available at almost every restaurant, so I'd eat my French fries and onion rings with tarter sauce. Even today I like tarter sauce with my fries better than catsup. When I go out to a restaurant for Gyro's and fries, I ask for extra Tzatziki sauce; because, I likes to dip my fries in it. I call the Tzatiki sauce, "TZ sauce," it's easier to pronounce and the waiters and waitresses always know what I'm asking for!

I miss the hamburger plate special on the menu. Sometimes for lunch at work, we'd go to the diner next door. I'd order the hamburger plate; it would come with 3 hamburgers (no bun,) green beans, French fries and they would pour gravy over everything. Yup, nothing likes a meal of gravy to go with all the fixings.

This diner located right next to work that I will not name was a "class act." George our electronic engineer went in there on afternoon and he caught one of the cooks cleaning his toe nails with a fork. He said something to the cook and he replied, "What? Do you think, I'm gonna pick the dirt from my toes with a spoon?" George was still hungry so he thought for a moment and figured eggs would be safe to eat. After all they are self-contained in a protective shell. How could the cook mess-up eggs. Well, he did. George told us he coughed without covering up his mouth and sprayed the eggs as he coughed. I don't remember if there were "A's" in the widows of restaurants back then?

The last time I was ordering my food with my work buddies at that diner, we heard the dishwasher in the back hacking and hocking attempting to clear something out of his throat? He (the dishwasher not a dishwasher as in an electrical unit that washes dishes) came out a little later after the food arrived and said to us, "Hey . . . you want gravy to go on your food?" We just laughed and said, "No!" I believe I know what the secret spice in his special bend of gravy was!

So when you're out to a restaurant remember: don't ask any question you don't want an answer too, plain is better and safer, and before you walk into the restaurant, is there an "A" in the window? A clean and new looking letter 'A' in a clean window better than an old and dirty letter 'A' and window; The 'A' could be an indicator on whether you may want to think about going somewhere else to eat, like home for instance.

Yep, one foot special order coming up!

Outta Sbzzz Mind

by SbWaitt

SbWaitt

"Here ya go...Our famous one foot pizza...It's hot and fresh; so, enjoy."

VALENTINES ELEPHANT

I DID MY BEST TO think of something cute and nice for Valentine's Day, with a cupid like theme. Elephants lighter than air with wings. You may wonder is this a little tiny cute miniature elephants or is it a huge full scale elephant, you know, a full grown elephants that weigh as much as a bus? Hmmm, how big are the arrows if it's the later? Ouch! "Harpoon away."

Maybe there is a world out here somewhere where elephants fly? What would there bone structure be like, are they hollow? Maybe it's a world with low gravity? I don't think I'd want to be underneath one, when it fly's over me!

We all look forward to Valentines Day? It's a special day for those in love. It's great to be in love. Do you know what love is? Can you describe love? What is your definition of love? Love is kind of abstract. Perhaps you can describe love by explaining what it isn't. Attempt to describe love to someone without using the love word. Then you may come close to your definition about love.

What? Not everyone has the same definition of love, well . . . I guess cupid is falling down on the job. Cupid is responsible for everyone to love one another or is that really Aphrodite's job? Hey, how does getting stuck with an arrow make someone want to fall in love? I'd think it would make you want to scream, yell, cry, or pass out . . . "Hey someone call 9-1-1!"

I've given out flowers, chocolates and gifts several times over the years. Only once did I ever receive flowers. I'm not complaining, I'm making a statement. These "one day a year" holidays, occasions or reminders of how we like to be treated all year round, is tough to live up too at times.

What would the world be like if we treated everyone as if it was Valentine's Day every day . . . ? Same goes for Christmas, thanksgiving, mother's day, father's day, birthdays, etc . . . yea, let's be kind a few days out of the year an treat everyone terrible the rest of the year. Well, the greeting card businesses and stores selling the cards like it. They don't even mind if you do treat people not so good because then you can buy "let's make up cards" because I'm sorry how I treated you.

It's good to know how your special friend, spouse, and/or person you have affection for likes to receive gifts and what kind of gifts they like to receive. Sounds crazy, however it goes smoother if you ask the other person what they like and take good notes or ask from time to time, a lot, because they may change their mind. It's ok to change one's mind. It's really great when a memo goes out to you about the change. It's not something that usually happens though. We live in a world we're we are supposed to be mind-readers. Ever hear the comment or reply after giving someone the wrong gift, "If you really loved me you'd know what I want!" I'm not a psychic so I ask.

Do you know how you like to give or receive special attention such as in the way of: special gifts, quality time together, tender touch, praise and acknowledgement, acts of service, giving of self, and/or creating a special environment for the setting and mood? This giving and receiving may change depending on if it's for a friend, co-worker, neighbor, relative, sweet heart, or associate. Again, asking is a good thing; so take good notes so you can remember when it's time to give a gift to that special someone.

Communication with understanding of each other works better than attempting to be a mind reader. In my younger years I didn't realize it was a good thing to ask, I thought it would come natural somehow? And you know what? It never did come natural. Did you ever give a gift because you would like to receive the gift as a gift? This may backfire on you. You may receive more than the gift you last gave if this is your standard mode of operation.

We are not in the business of changing people even though it would be nice if we all enjoyed the same stuff. Would you like to receive a gift of lipstick and perfume because she likes it . . . maybe if you were a girl!

Outta Sbzzz Mind

by Sb Waitt

SbWaitt

"NO WAIT,
CHIEF KNOWS WHAT SHE'S DOING!"

DURING MY DAYS OF THE navy I was a surface sonarman which is a very ocean orientated rate. My job was to hunt for submarines. Once I became a technician and added responsibility was to maintain the sonar equipment.

I was stationed on Combatant Ships, so at that time there were no women stationed on them; they are now with the more modernized-equality navy. It's a good thing! My interaction with women during in my stay in the navy was on my tours at shore duty. Regardless of being male or female aboard the ship a job has to be performed. The ship comes first, then the equipment, and finally the crew. There are no, "Oh that's good enough because you're a girl," stuff. The equipment must work correctly all the time.

Yes, something as simple as changing a light bulb was done the same way regardless of your sex. We all could be shocked or electrocuted if we didn't follow the safety rules. Some of the equipment had to be de-energized in order to perform certain tasks. High voltage loves to reach out to unsuspecting sailors that aren't paying attention. Where are talking about voltages that can knock you out and even fry you to death.

Ahhh, the life of a navy chief petty officer can be difficult at times we don't always want to step down and let the troops do the work. I enjoyed my time working my way up in ranks. My goals as an E-6 or below were to do what I could do without being told what to do. Other goals were to do the work and assure the petty officer in charge over me that if I need help I'll call you.

The best rank below an E-7 was petty officer second class (E-5) in my opinion. I got to do most of the technical work, I had some junior petty officer and seaman below me, and I usually only answered to my leading petty officer. Oh yes, once advancing in rank to 2nd class very little cleaning or chipping and painting work.

I enjoyed advancing to first class petty officer (E-6) however I really, really enjoyed and liked being a chief petty officer. Stay on the deck plates and make the rounds with your men in the division and coordinate with those that we depended on to support our division. I enjoyed being on the various ship board training teams. Training required extra hours when others went off the ship on liberty, yet it was fun, rewarding, and when we passed inspections the sensation was invigorating, I was jazzed, excited, happy, and couldn't wait for the next inspection!

The hard work paid off prior to refresher training, that's where the whole ship is in simulated battle drills for weeks at a time until we pass all our drills. The enjoyable part is when the evaluators select various individuals to be killed off . . . I was killed off numerous times so I had the pleasure to walk around freely and watch.

One of my favorite times was during fresh water wash down. This is where the crew breaks off in to teams and man the fire hoses to wash the salt off of the paint and equipment topside. I liked to dress in my oldest and grubbiest kaki-working uniform and go topside to help coordinate. I liked to stand in front of the hose team and point out areas when the guys missed spots. I gave them the opportunity to spray down the chief and I'd always say afterwards, "Good work men!" Sometimes they were a little apprehensive, yet I'd continue to point out areas near my feet or somewhere where the water would splash, drenches me, and wash the ship. The mission came first. A little play was always good, especially when intertwined with work.

I always found fun in what ever I did in the navy. The pleasure seemed to grow as the years went by. My warped sense of humor was good and came in handy at times in my opinion. The evaluators on board to grade the performance of the crew would pull me aside and tell me I was good for the morale of the ship and that I knew what I was doing when the time came for seriousness. Several asked me to talk to my detailer to become part of their training team. There was always something going on aboard a ship that I found to be interesting and entertaining. In my single years I didn't want to go to shore duty.' I truly would rather sail out to sea on deployment than be stationed on land.

Outta Sbzzz Mind by SbWaitt

"No, wait..Chief knows what she is doing."

OCCUPIED

THERE IS MORE THAN ONE way to become occupied in life. Octopi like to wrap around things and dominant. How have you been dominated over the years of your life? Do you become wrapped up in other people's affairs, business, and life, only to forget about your life? Sometimes the octopus is a reminder for us to slow down and think. Remember you don't have eight arms; it's hard to concentrate on more than one task at a time, and unwind yourself from all the little things that don't really matter.

Yes the tentacles have many little suction cups that are good at sucking, holding, not letting go! As you attempt to remove one arm another one tightens up. Once you free one arm from the tight grip, there are still seven more arms to deal with. As you reach to remove another tentacle he latches back with one with the arm you just unraveled. What you need is" help!"

Do you ask for help or do you let things become out of hand? We are not alone in this world. It is OK to ask for help. No one person has all the right answers, solutions, plans for successes, or has eight arms. I believed I had to do everything on my own and where did it get me? Asking for help is a hard pill to swallow when my pride, ego, desire to be right, and need to look good kick in and take control. I've messed-up many things in my life time because I had to do it all myself.

Being occupied feels like you have a ball and chain attached to your legs. Maybe you feel weights attached to your arms as well. Soon the mind becomes heavy, full of noise, and then the committee in your head starts to babble with voices all talking at the same time. It can be very confusing when you're not sure which direction to turn or which voice is in chsrge.

For years I attempted to fill out my taxes by myself. This isn't supposed to be hard in my mind. Well, I had great difficulties towards getting it all straight and correct. I'd mail in my return only to find I goofed! I usually had to pay. I don't mind paying my fair share. The problem is when I figured I'd receive a check back only to receive a notice that I owe. I felt like a failure when it came to meeting the April 15th dead line. I got to where I didn't want to file. I confided to a friend about my difficulties towards figuring out my own taxes. The suggestion was to have someone else do them for me. Huh, why do I have to pay for someone to do my stuff, because? I don't seem to have the knack for doing it correctly. I've had a tax accountant do my taxes for years since 1992. Having someone do for me makes life a little easier for me now! My time is freed up a bit and I don't carry the self-induced stress of failure. However I do have to look closer at the mail and put all the required stuff for the taxes in one pile.

I like to do for others and I disregard what needs to be done for me. I figure if I do for others I can ignore self, yet at "O dark Thirty" the voices keep me awake through the night. They nag me about what is not being accomplished. So the next day I'm tired, drag feet, and don't take care of self or those I'm responsible for in an adult, caring way.

Being occupied distracts us from becoming all we can be. We forget what fun and laughter feels like. Life becomes a challenge and at times we'd like to throw in the towel. I've said that we are here to be supportive of one another. I didn't always believe that reciprocation was part of the equation. Yes, be helpful and also ask for help when needed. Being helpful doesn't always mean you do everything for another. Helping involves two or more people, this include the person receiving help . . . It's good to help, when "asked," and sometimes we have to say "no" about helping others because I have things that must come first. Once they are accomplished then I'll help if needed.

I thought of being occupied while aboard a plane. I was waiting to use the restroom and waited and waited and waited. What was going on in there for the person in there to take so long? I was becoming impatient while and my mind wandered off while staring at the occupied sign by the door latch. Only one person came out. When I was finished with the restroom I went back to my seat and started doodling in my sketch book.

Outta Sbzzz Mind   by SbWaitt

Occupied

NO ONE BELIEVED ERWIN WHEN HE TOLD EVERYBODY THAT BIGFOOT LIKED TO STOP BY AT NIGHT FOR GRILLED HOTDOGS

WHAT I FORGOT TO MENTION is . . . They also like to sit around a fire while listening and singing to Cat Stevens music. After a couple hours of singing, Erwin went into the pantry and broke out the graham crackers, chocolate bars, and marshmallows so they could enjoy making and eating tasty S'mores. You didn't know Bigfoot likes to sing and eat S'mores? Well they do enjoy the taste of chocolate and they have a sweet voice. So when you make a Bigfoot friend you now have something to look forward too.

Usually Bigfoot likes to stay out of view and hide from people however, he has a good sense of character and felt Erwin was gentle and kind. They will always remain friends. Once they watched the fourth episode of Star Wars. Erwin noticed that his friend really enjoyed watching the movie; so, they made a night of it and watched the next two episodes. Bigfoot really enjoys the characters of Chewbacca and the Ewoks the best. He also liked eating buttered popcorn and drinking root beer. Occasionally Erwin paused the movie while they indulged in a gut-wrenching belching contest and you'll never guess who the champion was.

Erwin has been enrolled in guitar lessons. He'd like to see if he could teach Bigfoot to play a song or two when he knows more about making chords and his abilities improve. So for now Erwin is happy with the time he enjoys with his special friend.

I'd like to believe that we haven't found all the animals on our planet. So I'm a want-a-be Bigfoot believer. I record and watch all the TV shows I find about Sasquatch. I don't believe everyone that reports a sighting is untruthful. I think this is the most believable of all the unexplained creatures that people tell stories about. There is still a great deal of territory out there that is uninhabited by people with lots of wild life running free . . .

Maybe the face on Mars is really a face of Bigfoot! What, NASA proved there was no face on Mars? Your face might become a little eroded after a couple of million years of sand storms blowing in your eyes! These yeti creatures are they perhaps really Martians? Is it important how Sasquatch came into being or where they came from? Coexistence is what's important for now. People in general have a difficult time getting along with one another.

It's kind of neat when you do things that no one else believes you do, like Erwin. Possibly, he's not the favorite person in school when it comes to socialization, being picked for a sports team, or doing what everyone else does. He beats his own drum and at times he isn't even using a drum; he is learning to play the guitar. He's very happy and content. The special time he spends with his Bigfoot friend is cherished.

If others came around to see what Erwin is up too? The others wouldn't see anyone else around except Erwin. Bigfoot is very cautious and likes his privacy. Erwin knows if his friend doesn't show up there will be other times, because they have made a connection. He doesn't question why because they trusts one another as friends whole heartedly.

Being different is great. No one person has all the qualities that we enjoy or desire. The ways of others may not work for self. The key is to believe in self and not be afraid to walk down a different path that others walk. Erwin thinks outside of the sandbox. He's not content following. He may not see that he is a leader and a person with great qualities.

He knows right now he has a wonderful relationship going on. We are all unique in our own ways. Erwin is unique in being a friend. Unknowingly he transmits a frequency that is picked up from those that are receptive and open to new possibilities. What a quality in his personification to possess.

Yes the simple things in life can be wonderful memories and long lasting times of enjoyment. A hotdog, a S'more, and a song . . . Sounds like the making of a great time around the campfire or fireplace for years to come.

Outta Sbzzz Mind by Sb Waitt

"No one believed Erwin when he told everybody that Bigfoot liked to stop by at night for grilled hotdogs."

BILL ALWAYS BELIEVED THERE WAS
A SECRET MEANING WRITTEN IN THE STARS
AND ONE DAY HE WOULD FIND IT!

LIKE BILL, I'M LOOKING FOR the hidden meanings in things. I'd be jazzed if I found some old authenticated writing on a stone that I turned over while walking somewhere. To find proof of an alien existence is at the top of my want to find list. I'm hooked on the playback feature on my TV. It takes me twice as long to watch shows about Egypt tombs, UFO's, ancient explorers, Atlantis, Stonehenge, and new discoveries with archaeology findings; the list goes on and on.

Look hard enough and you will find what you are looking for regardless of where you look! Look for the fun stuff! Look for the comical stuff! Look for the good stuff! We seem to easily find and see the bad stuff. It's all about perception and attitude with the action of choice. If we find one positive to offset the negativity why not key on the positive. Life is better with a good outlook than the opposite. One good point dis-proves all those things we believe are always bad. We may find that the word 'always' is not true. So, be careful when you say and use the word 'always' and 'always' is a hard standard to live by.

On my wall in my living room I have a banner that I printed out from my computer . . . **HAPPINESSISNOWHERE**. What do you see? Bill sees the stars. He looks for new worlds. He wants to make contact. He also likes to eat pizza. Most of us do. About the only thing I don't want on a pizza are anchovies. There is no such thing as half a pizza with anchovies. The little fish always find a way to migrate to the other side of the pizza. Well, I don't want beets or collard greens on my pizza either or shampoo, woodchips, chewing gum, paint, ink, or things that we don't usually eat. Think outside of the box and what will you find?

You never know who is looking over your shoulder and watching you from a far or up close? Sometimes we become tunnel-visioned, miss the big picture, and deprive ourselves of new pleasures and experiences. I believe we are being visited and I want to find convincing proof!

Seek and you may find pizza or something else to your liking. Take things for granted or keep your eyes closed and you miss out! I've missed out on many things because I chose to stay in the mindset; that what I believed was right and wouldn't allow another idea as a possibility.

I rode a small rollercoaster as a child just before entering third grade. I was frightened and screamed. I didn't ride another one until Navy Boot Camp liberty at Marriott's Great Adventure theme park in the summer of 1976. All the prior years I believed I was not suppose to ride roller coasters because they are scary. Yet, I've watched people and friends ride them with enjoyment for years. I planted the thought in my brain and held onto it. I do have a fear of heights; I've yet to conquer it. I ride on a rollercoaster and sing load on the way up. Once we start rolling downwards I start screaming . . . I found if I scream going down the first hill I can breathe going up the next. Now I find that its fun to be scared! I've parachuted and when my eyes are even with the horizon I would close them, feel the wind to my face' and prepare for a blind landing . . . Once I had a perception of height the fear would kick in. I choose not to parachute anymore after marrying and having children I had one accident and didn't want to risk a more severe one . . . I use to jump with the old style rigs so when I landed I would go into a 5 point roll.

When I fly, I sit deep into my seat and close my eyes during take-off. After a minute or so when I feel comfortable I open them. I enjoy looking down at the ground at a high altitude; it looks like a huge picture and I don't sense the height anymore. I trust the pilot and airplane so I don't ride with constant fear. The landings are the same way. I look away and/or close my eyes until the plane bounces a few times on the runway and the retro-rockets kick in . . . At least I believe the deceleration is from retro-rockets. I'm glad that we don't stop like in the days of the Flintstones, "Everybody, this is the captain speaking . . . Please prepare to stomp your feet down on the runway and push until the plane comes to a complete stop!" Ahhh, we have landed, "Happiness is now here!"

Bill always believed that there was a secret written in the stars and one day he would find it!

"WHY DID MOSES PART THE RED SEA?"
"AHHH, TO GET TO THE OTHER SIDE?"

I ALWAYS ENJOYED CHICKEN JOKES as a child, teenager, and still do! As well, I got a hoot out of elephant jokes. Dry, dumb, silly, or any other kind of humor I enjoy.

Depending on where the sea was parted would determine if there was a wall of water growing on onside and on the other side the water could keep running its course and disappear out of sight. The part could be miles wide before the wall of mounting water was aloud to collapse and go back to normal. If they crossed where the bottom contour was at a low point then there could have been water on both sides of the part while crossing. Or, God wanted the spectacular effect! So regardless he had water on both sides of the parted sea! God has a sense of humor and is in control so I go for the spectacularism . . . Too bad Charlton Heston isn't around today, he'd know! That's probably a secret he shared with God. Yea, they laugh about now from time to time. If you don't think God has a sense of humor make plans and tell God your plans; see what happens to those plans. We may not get what we want however we usually get what we need; hey isn't that in a song too?

Now why chicken jokes . . . Hmmm, not a clue. I believe they act dumb so we have to feed them. No, that's not true . . . They are dumb. Ever eat a smart chicken? That's my answer.

So, I trust the God of my understanding has a sense of humor and will not strike me down with lightening if some of my humor involves Him. He may send locus my way, not lightening. A few minutes ago I was being overthrown by ants and didn't realize it. You see I had my soft drink on a coaster behind me away from the computer and keyboard. Occasionally, I'd reach back; take a drink, the set the glass down on the coaster. Anyway, I don't always inspect the glass before I swallow and drink some of the contents of the glass. I wish I had. After a couple more swallows I started to notice an ant or two by the computer monitors. I grab a Kleenex and started pressing on the ants. The trail leads me all the way back to my glass! Yuck . . . Toothpaste and mouthwash is a wonderful thing. So isn't bug spray . . . Perhaps He knew what I was going to write about and sent me ants instead of locus.

One of my favorite biblical jokes is, "How many animals did Moses bring onto the ark?" I think when the ark was completed the animals where either all baby animals or God stopped the growth process until they got to the other side of the rainbow and the waters resided. Maybe think out side of the box a little. If God wants something to happen, it will, why not . . . If'n She/He can create, I'm sure She/He can do a lot of other things whether we want to believe it or not.

If you were the creator, how would you have created this world or your world? What would be different, similar or the same. Would you have a sense of humor about all the crazy creations running around the planet thinking they have all the answers when, in all actuality, they don't have a clue! Will you let them do there own thing?

In my world, pizza, popcorn and ice-cream would not be fattening! We'd eat French fries with tartar sauce. Beets would only be fed to animals. Guys wouldn't go bald, grow nose and ear hairs, or have to clip the toe nails. At the age of 30 we'd receive our third set of teeth (not the false kind.) Third time is a charm. Oh yea almost forgot, farts and sweat wouldn't stink! I'm thinking about warm weather snow that is not slippery and only sticks to grass and trees and it will only accumulate a total of 1 inch on the roads and sidewalks to create a beautiful scene when people take pictures.

Outta Sbzzz Mind by Sb Waitt

"Why did Moses part the Red Sea?. Ahhh, to get to the other side?"

BABY BOTTLE

A BABY AND A BOTTLE, a baby with a bottle, a baby with a bottle on their head, a baby drinking from a bottle, a baby in a bottle, a bottle bottling up a baby sitting in the bottle, "ohhh! A baby bottle." I say out loud. Girl children play with small baby bottles while having fun with their dolls. My baby bottle picture might make a cute little knick knack, if you like knick knacks. I wonder where the word "knick-knack" came from? Who first said, "Oh, what a cute knick-knack?" and why the word knick-knack? I recall the word Knick-Knack was the name of a villain's assistant in one of those secret agent movies.

Seeing as I'm on a word kick . . . I'd like to know, what a patty whack is? That phrase plants the images of receiving spanking. What does it have to do with giving a dog a bone? Do you remember the song and how it goes?

As a parent, there were many nights of waking up to the sounds of a baby crying out of hunger or wet diapers. Yes, I've boiled a few and change a few in my days and nights as dad! That's, boil the bottle and change diapers not the other way around! Most of the time it was boil a bottle and throw away the dirty diaper. Ahhh, disposable is the way to go.

Perhaps a large baby bottle device might make for an interesting crib, playpen, car seat or floating device for the swimming pool. Yes, it would have to be well ventilated. It kind of looks like a spaceship, perhaps when superman was a baby, this was the original design for his escape rocket from the planet krypton!

It could be good for time outs after the child throws their tantrum and continues to cry. It could come with a muffler device to reduce the volume of the heavy crying. I'm not saying place the child in the bottle and leave town. I was always close by while the crying was going on. I made sure there were no injuries with the crying. Children are our future and comforting the child is important. A crying child can work-up an appetite or become very tired; they expend a lot of energy if we are not successful in calming the child down.

I believe today that I am a much better Grand Parent than I was a dad. I did my best, if only I could turn back the clock and do a few things differently. I have two wonderful children I am so thankful for, I am blessed. I had lots of help in the early years after my wife died. Cindy was a wonderful wife, person and my best friend. My brother Jim and his wife Louise helped raise my children for 5 years before I retired from the navy and found a home in San Diego. Single parenting was scary as we all have been told and found out. Children don't come with an instruction book. My buddy Howard had a big part too. I stayed with him for 3 months with my children before finding a home. He then moved in with us for about a year.

I do have the pleasure of watching one of my grandchildren before and after school. During his learning how to read period, I'd tape words of things around the house above the item and on the walls such as: lamp, picture, cat door, fan, wall, clock, mask, etc . . . I still have some of the words on the walls today. I don't have whatever it takes to remove them; they are reminders of good memories.

Each of my children made a mask at some point in their school years. I have them hung on the wall next to their respective picture. I was going to plaster them and smooth them into the wall however when I become old and senile, looking at their mask and pictures wherever I end up may help me to have lapses of remembrance-memories that I will cherish before the mind clouds over again.

One of my nieces said to me, "Uncle B, when you become old and senile you'll act and be normal like everyone else!" Yea, I dance to the beat of a difference set of tambourines! Whoops, there's that 'normal' word snuck into a sentence at the beginning of this paragraph. May you beware of the word 'normal' or at least think about the word. Do you know what normal is? Well, that's another time and another story.

Outta Sbzzz Mind   by SbWaitt

Baby Bottle

CONTOUR DRAWING NUMBER I

IF YOU EVER ENROLL IN a college for a class for art lessons, eventually you'll be taught the contour drawing method. I like to call this The Helen Keller Method of Drawing or The Seeing Eye Dog Drawing Technique! Yes, it's an eye opener designed, to stimulate your eye hand coordination without watching your paper.

Step one, look at the subject. **Step two**, look at the paper. **Step three**, look at the subject and determine where you want to start drawing your first line. **Step four**, Place your drawing implement at the precise spot you want to start from (don't move your hand yet) and look at the subject without moving your pencil, pen, crayon or whatever you are using to draw with. **Step five**, keep your eye on the subject and move your drawing device the way you see the first line is to be created without looking at anything other than the subject. When you believe you have accomplished this task of drawing without looking you may cautiously lift your hand that is holding the drawing tool from the paper. Now that this line is drawn you may start step 6! **Step six**, look at subject to determine where the next line will start from and repeat the process over and over until you believe your picture is finished.

How do you master this technique? "Practice, practice, practice," and when you're done practicing, practice some more, more, more and more! It's fun, it's great, it's what a great artist does, so I've been told. It's a way of removing interpretation from your art work to capture realism. Not my favorite technique! I believe this technique is why people buy cameras, scanners, and drop art classes. Well, whatever you do . . . Don't drop the art class.

Remember the classes you take in school and college is to expand your horizons. You will be pushed and pulled into new directions of art. You will learn things that will enhance your appreciation of art. The art instructor is there for you to grow from. Suck their minds dry of what why know about art, drawing, painting, etc . . . and then you will emerge wiser, better, improved, honed, seasoned and above all, brain dead . . . This outcome is short lasting, you will recover. Yes, you will now see that your art instructor has opened your mind to a world of art you may never have realized existed or wanted to know existed. Appreciate that!

Art appreciation is the appreciation of everyone that ever went to art class, school, or college before self. We appreciate the torture, torment and hard work that went into your studies and abilities to improve self and in becoming the artist that you are today, now, presently!

I had a tough time with the word torture. My New England accent is still there and I still have a terrible time with the spelling of some (a lot of) words I pronounce as a New Englander. I even befuddle the spell check in my computer . . . I spelt it, "tourcher," all the words that popped up didn't look right to me. We take the letter "R" out of some words and add and "R" in words that don't have this letter such as, "Lets gwet a pizzer with Peppahs," or, "I'll meetya at the bahn at a quateh of fouwah. I'll wait fowah a half houwah befoah I leave at qwuatah aftah fowah." Translations: "Let's go eat a pizza with peppers," and "I'll meet you at the barn at a quarter of four. I'll wait for a half hour before I leave at quarter after four."

People out here say, "You talk with a Bostonian accent!" I reply, "I don't talk with an accident!" The New England drawl comes out the strongest when I'm in a hurry, nervous, excited, or distracted.

Today I use some of those techniques that I felt I was being tortured with and said, "I'll never use this form of drawing once I leave this class . . . Learning some of this stuff is a waste of time . . ." There were days when I was very co-operative and there were days when all I wanted to do was leave and go draw the assignment, my way . . . then there were days when I wanted more, more, more . . . School, whether it is High School or College is a rollercoaster ride, It's up, down, fast, bumpy, may want to hurl, it stops, you thrown this way and that way . . . Then you run back in line to ride it again.

Last thought; what does expand your horizon mean? Perhaps tonight we will have a vision!

Contour Drawing Number I

LE SPAM FOR WOMEN

THIS IDEA CAME TO ME while I was in a relationship seminar. The facilitator asked, "What do you want in your relationship now or in a future relationship?" I replied, "She must like spam!"

I'm not sure why women wear the scent of colognes and perfumes they do? I'd believe a perfume with the aroma of turkey cooking in the over would be the scent to allure men in. Now add a lipstick that tastes like grave and "O-BOY," Where do you want to go tonight baby!!!! Another good fragrance would be bacon with country gravy or spam lipstick. However, I'm a guy and I probably have it all wrong why ladies wear their special selected scent they wear? What I least like about the colognes and perfumes is the taste terrible if you kiss a girl where the scent is applied and I usually feel the scent on my skin before I smell it. Now the fruit scented hair wash is appealing to me . . . I think they wear the stuff because they like the fragrance . . . Maybe it's time to ask why they wear the scents they do . . . I'm sure the answer will destroy men's ego. Such is life. You know what; now's a good time to open up a can of spam!

So, spam . . . It's good to eat any time of day or night. What does not go good with spam???? I like to brown the outside to a golden brown color. It will then give me the desired sensation of crunchy-ness when I bite into the tasty delight. Occasionally I coat my spam with a blend of brown sugar, mustard, and vinegar . . . Mmmmm good, it gives the kitchen a good manly cooking aroma. I also like it right out of the can as is. I like classic spam, not turkey or low sodium spam. I'm still debating the easy to open pull tab can thing. It just doesn't feel right. If it's not broken . . . Don't, fix it!

On the cooking shows I've watched chefs cook with the wonderful delight out of the can. So if a chief will cook with it, why wouldn't you? All so, if you enjoy a Hawaiian vacation, spam is popular on the Islands.

So there was a time in my non-single days that I was asked to only cook spam when I was home alone. I was also asked to open the windows and turn on the fans while cooking and afterwards to clear the air. The wonderful fragrance lingers for a long time, specially if you leave the pan on the stove with just a little water added, after the spam is removed from the cooking instrument.

I'm thinking about a line of spray Le Spam scented air fresheners. They would be a great guy item to buy. How about, a Le spam air freshener for the car! It would look just like the can and I'd hang it off of the front rear view mirror. Yep, so don't forget about hanging one these great smelling beauties to enhance the ambiance though out the car like in the backseat somewhere. I can taste the aroma now, sweet.

So girls, whose going to be first to wear and use this great line of new products designed to lure in the men? You'll be in the center limelight all evening anywhere you go. You'll never be on the sideline again at a singles dance. Your home phone will be ringing off the night stand by your bed and your phone recorder will be full. On the back of your business cards add, "I'm a le Spam girl." It's guaranteed to place your name at the top of any interview list.

Make sure you read the disclaimer along the left side of the ad on the drawing; it's very important. Be ready and be prepared. Please don't judge men to harshly when they actually drool in your presence. You're going to ruin a man's shirt or two and put men's necks into a brace. The pied piper never had it so good! You walk anywhere and men will follow! You'll never be lonely again! You might consider buying a watch dog and/or using a heavy-fashionable walking stick.

Le spam products will guarantee that your eyes will see; a whole new and exciting world that never before have you ever seen and experienced.

Le Spam coming to stores everywhere!

Hey, I just had a great Idea . . . instead of moth balls in the closet . . . Spam Balls! Nothing else needs to be said . . . Spam balls

Outta Sbzzz Mind   by Sb Waitt

Le Spam for women

KOO KOO KA CHOO

WHAT WOULD IT BE LIKE to have tusks? I'm sure life would have been different over the years. Can you whistle with tusks or play the Clarinet? I'm sure the Tuba would be challenging! I believe it's hard to pucker-up with those long spikes sticking out of your mouth and it may hurt at times. Maybe eventually we would either have decided to file the down or remove them all together during the early stages of our development. It seems like they would get in the way of our way of life today.

"I am the Walrus . . . I am the Walrus, koo koo ka choo" Whenever I hear this song play by the Beatles on the radio or I place the Cd in the player t jam out with some tunes, some thoughts and memories come to mind . . .

While Stationed aboard my 3rd ship, USS Harry E Yarnell CG-17 I had a run in with a few division officers. One of my Favorites was Mr. Zamparelli, We, the sailors that where part of the ASW Division, called him Mr. "Z". He was a Woody Allen look-a-like and times, sound alike. He is the only line office I know that majored in film and theater, at least that's the impression I received about him. He knew all about the ins and outs of movies and actors, and also enjoyed music.

He was a little off the wall as officers were, in a good way. A very independent thinker and quick whiter in his laid back way . . . He had Zampisms and I had Sbologies. So it was enjoyable to listen to him. He'd say, "Waitt, I believe my Zampisms will win out over your Sbologies before one of us leaves the ship!" Those 'isims' are our outward expression about how life runs and operates, our witticisms, beliefs, mantras, and those inward things and thoughts that drive us when no one will support us . . .

Out at sea and import there was always someone on duty or on watch 24 hours a day, 7 days a week (on the days we advanced the clock it was 23hours and the days we retarded the clock it was 25 hours however I'm sure you figured that out for yourself!) One day he asked me to specifically be the one to wake him up for the 4-8 watch in the morning. He instructed me and said, "When you come to my stateroom to wake me up, I want you to say, "Who are you!" He said he would reply, "I am the walrus!" I wasn't supposed to leave until he also added, "Koo Koo Ka Choo, Koo Koo Ka Choo!" If we want to be relieved from our watch stations, wake-up is very important. We'd usually have to check our reliefs a couple of times and make sure their feet where on deck. Only once, during my time of making the round for wake-ups did someone climb back into his rack.

The first time I ever woke up and officer for watch was aboard my first ship USS Gray FF-1054. I was standing my first watch as Messenger of the Watch during the mid-watch (midnight to 4 in the morning.) Now, to this day I still say my Petty Officer of the Watch told me when I go below to wake up Mr. Bloomburg I was to bang on the door as hard as I could! So I bangs on this door as hard as I could and it seemed like seconds later . . . this sleepy-eyed officer opens the door and is standing in his underwear and bare feet, tendering back and forth a little off balanced, and he's screaming at me, "WHAT DO YOU THINK YOUR DOING!" I calmly said, "It's time for watch sir I was sent to wake you up." I turned and walked away to the sound of the door slamming behind me . . .

I told the Petty Officer of the Watch what I did. He laughed at me and said, "Nooooooo! I said not to bang on the door." At that time we were both laughing. When Mr. Bloomburg arrived at the quarter deck to assume the watch, he eyed me up and down, in and out. Yet he never said a word to me. He wasn't late for watch. We actually developed a pretty good working relationship during our stay aboard the Gray.

"I am a Walrus,' what could that mean. What do you want it to mean? Who are you? Who am I? We are all someone's friend, relative, co-worker, associate, next door neighbor . . . We may have many titles in life or other ways of defining our self. The ones I like today are when I make 'I Am' Statements: I am an artist, I am worthy, I am valuable, I am creative, I am thoughtful, I am loved, I am supportive, I am a dreamer, I am musical, maybe even . . . I am a walrus . . . and the list goes on and on. I challenge you to write down as many I am statements as you can. Listen to other people and hear what they say. Add to your list all the positive things you are and want to be. Yes you can add all the 'I Am' a brother, sister, uncle and all the other titles associated with being a relative, friend, or worker with people . . .

I enjoy finding music about 'Who I Am' and who I want to be. We are able to find more music if you can drop the male/female barrier and listen to the message only. Here's some that I like: "Bitch," by Meredith Brooks; "I Am," by Hilary Duff; "I Believe I Can Fly," by R. Kelly; "I Just Can't wait to be King," by Jason Weaver; "I want to Know What Love Is," by Foreigner; "Soul Man," Blues Brothers; "True Colors," by Cindy Lauper and the list grows as I listen to more music. Music is a great way to reinforce who we are.

Outta Sbzzz Mind   by Sb Waitt

Koo Koo Ka Choo

WHILE IRONING OUT THE DIFFERENCES IN A RELATIONSHIP, THE SKELETONS, GHOSTS, AND DEMONS POP-UP.

RELATIONSHIPS WOULD BE SO MUCH, more, easier if we were all born with devices that would tell us when we meet someone if we are compatible as friends, neighbors, associates, spouses, co-workers. Then all we would need to know if we are on the same page, same book, same language, same edition, hmmmm same planet.

Did your current relationship begin as you thought it would? Were both of you truthful, honest, and authentic? Did you still have skeletons, ghosts, and demons hiding even after you walked down the aisle, stood in front of the justice of the peace, minister, priest or whoever performed the wedding ceremony. Did you hear the music behind you after you were joined together, thinking, "everything is gonna be alright now!" You're relationships are at their best in the early stages because I, you, we want to look good to one another. We keep thinking, "things are gonna get better.

Yep there was/is more to discuss and keep dreaming that, perhaps it won't surface, they will never find out, we're married now they will understand, I'll be OK if he/she have some things to tell me that he/she hasn't told me as of yet! Bummer . . .

Talk and talk about all you can think about before the commitment stage. Then ask more questions. Ask your friends for questions to ask. Have your friends ask their friend about questions to ask. Ask, ask, ask . . . You have that right. There is no question that you can think of that you're not allowed to ask.

That ring on your finger does not give you mind reading powers. What you're not sure of . . . ask, if you think something is bothering them . . . ask. If you ask a question that deserves a yes or no answer and you receive something in between, ask again and again and again! If they are not willing to give you a straight answer then the alarms will be ringing in your head right about now and every time thereafter you get a answer that doesn't fit the question, the voices in your head of doubt become louder.

Black and white questions are not answered with gray answers. If they are, what are you, me, we going to do? Justify in our head the right answer they meant to say? No! Take the next answer they give whether or not their answer answers the question you asked? No! Shut-off the bells, whistles, and alarms screaming in your ear? No! Consider something isn't working here? Yes!

Always praise and acknowledge their honesty. The object is to promote a safe environment for truthful and honest answers, regardless if you like the answer or not. Keep the relationship flowing with love, care and understanding. Nothing has to be terminal until you reach those things that you cannot tolerate, the pain is unbearable, and there is no compromise or change. So keep an open mind and see what happens. Change is a possibility if you, I, they, or we want change. Forcing change is not a possibility.

Do you know the difference between truth and honesty? A person can be truthful and leave out the details they don't want you to hear. Honesty includes all the little details. Example: I received a speeding ticket last night because the cop was out to fulfill his quotas. I was only going 5 miles over the speed limit. What wasn't said is, they blew a .1 on the breathalyzer, you didn't pass the sobriety test, the police officer gave you a break, and he let you off with a speeding ticket because he felt you could drive home safely!

What stuff are you holding onto secretively that is causing separation in your current relationship? Why don't you think they will understand? Professional help is an option not a sentence; it's helpful to have an unbiased opinion when you don't feel a solution together will happen. Everyone deserves a 2nd chance or more if the other party is willing. Starting over fresh, new, and honest is a possibility and works if you work at it.

I'm not a relationship counselor. I had my difficulties in my marriages. I would love to have a do over. My thinking did get in the way sometimes. In my second marriage I eventually wanted to be right more than married. I still love that girl very much.

Today I'm working on having a better relationship with myself. When I start doing this, maybe then I can be a partner in a relationship. It takes 100% from each party to make it work. I do have a skeleton hanging in my closet as I type. Sometimes when a new guest comes over my house and is looking for the bathroom; they open up the closet door and I hear a scream. It's a Halloween skeleton I leave hanging in my closet as a reminder to be truthful, honest, and authentic.

I also have a placard on my wall made out of El Toro poop-poo. It's a reminder not to talk and spread the bull around with people. While spreading the fertilizer around I'm not being authentic and I might then think strongly about brushing my teeth. I'm having a nasty case of locomotive breath!

Outta Sbzzz Mind by Sb Waitt

While ironing out the differences in a relationship, the skeletons, ghosts, and demons pop-up.

A SCENE OUTTA THE TARZAN MOVIE
WE DIDN'T SEE

I NEVER READ ANY OF the original books by Edgar Rice Burroughs; however, as a child I enjoyed watching the Tarzan movies, TV show, and occasional comic book. I liked how he swung through the trees, gave a jungle howler to the animals, and could defeat any animal in the jungle that would attack or challenge his dominance. After watching these shows I wanted a chimpanzee for a pet and the ability to communicate with the animals. Sometimes as a child, my neighborhood friends and I would play Tarzan up in the woods. I was never good at climbing trees so I never played the part of Tarzan. Any time any of us would swing from a rope we always sang out the Tarzan howler regardless of what we were doing or playing.

The thought of running around bare foot hurts my feet today. I never could build up the callousness of playing too long in my bare feet. I enjoyed being barefoot in the summer, specially at camp or the beach. I'm sure there are lots of stuff on the ground of the jungle that could pierce the foot and hinder one's ability to walk later in life. In today's society shoes are still not impervious to nails and real sharp objects. I've pulled spikey things out of my feet from wearing sneakers or flip flops over the years and limped around till the foot healed.

Tarzan always outsmarts the hunters and poachers and kept the interests of the animals first regardless of his personal relationship. The lion may have been king; however, he was and is Lord of the Jungle.

One of my favorite spoofs on the story line was and still is the cartoon George of the Jungle. This is an animated series produced by Jay Ward and Bill Scott, who created The Rocky and Bullwinkle Show. The show is amusing to both children and adults; even the shows' theme song is fun to listen too over and over. If ya never watched them, give em a watch or two you may discover a new fun cartoon. I remember when at movie theaters there used to be a cartoon or two before the main movie. I believe, George of the Jungle, would be a great cartoon to remake and show before the main feature.

I've wondered and pondered what it would be like to be raised by apes or as in the case of Tarzan, gorillas to be specific. The human child is one of the most vulnerable beings on the face of the earth. They must be cared for by their parent for years before they can function on their own.

Watching wild pack animals giving birth on the science shows amaze me . . . Within hours or less after the newborns breath their first breathe and open their eyes within their hostile environment, their only chance to survive is; if, they can keep pace with the main pack they were born into . . . Keep up or die that's your only chance. If a young animal lags behind they become lost, die of starvation, or become prey to an stronger animal and fall victim to the needs of the food chain.

A small infant baby is pampered from day one. Milk feed, diapers, a place of comfort to sleep, late night feedings, being rocked and sung to, and all the other little things to make him or her feel wanted and loved.

Then there is Tarzan . . . yep he was milk feed alright. Then later he wasn't eating bottled or homemade baby food that you or I ate. When the time came for solid food he was eating pre-chewed bugs, insects, and leaves. On a good day to me he might be feed some pre-chewed fruit and vegetables. I'm sure he received the comfort and love from his adopted mother. I wonder how much more special she treated him. After all she had to notice he wasn't a gorilla and he must have failed miserably at climbing and clinging to trees and vines. I never researched what natural food a gorilla eats that isn't compatible to the humans' digestive system. Can one truly live without Milk shakes, burgers and fries? I pretty sure I remember those three food items in Maslow's hierarchy of needs. They were right at the top of the pyramid illustration. Believe it or not "Catsup" was not included, it's considered a luxury. Perhaps it's time for a 21st century up date of that diagram. I prefer Chocolate milk shakes and cheese burgers; yet again, they are another luxury item.

A few stories come to mind about feral children raised by non-human parents. The Epic of Gilgamesh was one of the first books written and had a character by the name of Enkidu and was raised by animals and ignorant of human society. Then there is the story of the brothers Romulus and Remus who were raised by a wolf; they became the founders of the city of Rome. A third story The Jungle Book by Rudyard Kipling had a child named Mowgli. He was lost by his parents in the Indian jungle during a tiger attack. Mowgli was adopted by the wolves, who named him Mowgli the Frog because of his lack of fur and his nature to not sit still. There are many other stories; however these are the ones that come to mind.

If you research the Internet you can find several accounts of wild children found and brought back into the edge of society. None of the children returned to civilization seem to be able to adjust to what they must believe, perhaps, is human captivity. I wonder if they ever saw their own reflection out in the wild and if they did, did they think that is who they really are.

Outta Sbzzz Mind   by SbWaitt

A scene outta the Tarzan movie we didn't see.

WILL, SMITH . . .
AND THE ORIGINAL MEN IN BLACK

THERE WAS AN EPISODE OF Lost in Space; titled, "Invaders from the Fifth Dimension," Doctor Smith was transported into an alien space ship. The aliens were in need of repairing there damaged computer system. They figured a human brain would do nicely. Doctor Smith convinced the aliens that there was a better brain than his that would work more efficiently. Yep, you guessed it, Will Robinson! In this show the aliens where only seen as heads, their bodies were in the blacked out for the floating head effect. As time goes on I forget that alien hands are seen from time to time positioned above the control; I'm reminded every time I re-watch this episode. Maybe the bodies of the aliens where in some kind of devise that transported live sustaining energy to the heads; when various body parts are needed, they think it and they appear. This could be a more efficient way of travel when you have superior mind capabilities.

I'm also a Doctor Who fan. The doctor's ship is called a Tardis and it looks like a police call box from London England. What the Tardis and the alien ship from Lost in Space have in common is they are bigger on the inside than how they appear on the outside. There have been other shows where the inside of things is not proportional to the outside; however that was not originally designed that way.

Over the three seasons the inside of the Jupiter II expanded. The pilot episode of the ship has one level. In season one and two the ship has two levels and a mystery room where the Chariot is stowed. What's new in season three, the ship expands with an operational space pod and a third deck for the power core. The one room I don't remember ever seeing is a bathroom and shower. It's gotta be there somewhere? There are ways to explain the changes. Possibly they set down on a world with space travel technology and they helped to modify the ship with an overhaul.

In my writings of future Lost in Space stories. The newer Jupiter ships are bigger in design. I'd think room is important for long voyages into space. Being able to have some alone time and privacy will help to maintain good relations over the months or years. Can you imagine being cooped up in tight quarters with the same people day in and day out without a break? The thirst for fresh conversations and new faces will grow as time moves on, only to settle for quietness and solitude.

I enjoy watching shows and movies or reading stories involving things from another dimension. It's out of our realm of realism. It opens the doorways of other possibilities. The mind expands into a different thought process. Thinking outside the box is what I admire most about science fiction and that there is a possibility that it may become fact one day.

It would be more economical an environmentally friendly if we could build homes that only look as if they have 500 square feet to the house like structure and yard. Imagine a small bungalow in appearance with 10,000 square feet or more of living space inside, with all the futuristic technology to make life better. This home can be equipped with; house cleaning robots, holographic fun rooms, self-cleaning and unbreakable dishes, and a sound system that would rival Carnegie hall. The possibilities in home design are only limited by one's mind. Yep hurry up and make a functional halo-deck device for home use. Soon you'll be scaling the mountains of the Himalayas, exploring the Moon and Mars, scuba diving, parachuting or any other idea you can think of to have fun without leaving your home.

Perhaps the aliens from the fifth dimension will stop over for a visit, have a drink coffee, stay for dinner, or indulge with you . . . a good head massage? Have you been visited in the middle of the night by aliens? May your visits have been pleasant ones? I dream of friendly visitation from beyond our solar system and would really like to be the one that makes the contact for the entire world to see. No way can we be the only life in our Galaxy and beyond. Come on ET stop by, put your feet up for a spell and sit by the fire, we'll pop some corn, make S'mores, sing songs together, and tell ascary story or two. Maybe Erwin and Bigfoot will stop by, to join in the fun?

In the spirit of the great endings of each episodes of Lost in Space

TO BE
CONTINUED
NEXT WEEK!
SAME TIME,
SAME CHANNEL

Outta Sbzzz Mind by Sb Waitt

Will, Smith....And the original men in black

SOMETIMES IN LIFE WE BECOME OCCUPIED WHEN WE LEAST EXPECT IT.

SO YOU'RE AT SEA SCUBA diving around sunken ships. The warm water is clear with great visibility and there is thousands of colorful fish all around. You and your dive buddy are slowly swimming around near the bottom. You spot the wreck and see fish entering though an opening. You reach out to your buddy and point. Together you swim in that direction over colorful corral. It's and easy swim there is hardly and current to fight. You're first to what could be a possible entrance and discover that the opening is a big porthole with the glass knocked out. You grab the outer rim of the porthole and pull yourself in just enough to look inside and assess the compartment you'll swim into once you determine it's safe. Little did you realize you where about to be 'occ-u-pied.'

I bet you didn't think that an octopus was lumbering around the galley of a sunken ship filling up pie shells with whip cream so he/she could have the pleasure of drilling you in the face with a bunch of pies. You see octopuses are smart, cleaver, and patient. He was aware that divers like to explore old relics such as rusted out ships on the bottom of the sea. You were targeted and once the pies were tossed at you, he started laughing, released a massive cloud of ink, and then jetted away never to be caught or seen.

When we are preoccupied in life we miss out. We don't enjoy or see everything that is going on around us, however who'd of ever thought that we'd be attacked by an Octopus with whip cream. He didn't see it coming. He was having too much fun. Can we ever have too much fun? Life is so short and precious. Have fun while you're here and don't take life to serious; because, no one gets out of life alive.

Have you ever scuba dived? It's fun and there is in illusion of flying when the water is clear. While breathing, the sounds of Darth Vader from Star Wars come to mind. My room mate at the time during Sonar "C" School was Mike L. and we participated and completed a scuba dive certification course together. The two of us for the first time swam in the open ocean as a scuba diver by the Coronado Islands (That's of the coast of San Diego.) That was in 1978/79 time frame and is a great memory.

The water was a little cloudy that day. Our entire scuba class was about 25 or so of us plus the instructor and some extra qualified helpers. We all were checked out by the dive master before we were allowed to swim off with our buddy. We jumped into the water, followed the chain from the boat about 50 feet to the bottom; where Bob was ready to inspect and test us on our under water diving skills for the last time. The test it wasn't anything that we hadn't experienced before in the pool. He's flooded our mask, turned off one of our bottles of air, and took off a weight belt . . . Only difference is we worked as a team at the bottom of the ocean instead of a swimming pool.

I remember sitting on the bottom looking up. I'd take-in a breath of air from the regulator, hold my breath while I reached to temporarily remove the mouth piece; I'd then blow out and make a donut shaped air bubble. I was amazed by this. Of course I'm easily amused at times!

There were these things soaring by us, inches away from our face mask. Then one of these things stopped about a foot away from me and stared at me. We both looked at each other for about 3 or 4 seconds. The thing was a seal. There were hundreds of them. They were curious and if you let them do there own thing all went well. Once they had their fill, of the scuba man swimming in there neck of the ocean, they went back to swimming, hunting for food, and sun bathing on the rocks. I'm sure the seals do other things when humans are not around like singing, dancing, and riding bicycles. That ball balancing thing is over rated. I didn't notice any big red balls on the rocks where they were playing and enjoying the day.

Outta Sbzzz Mind   by SbWaitt

Sometimes in life we become occupied when we least expect it.

GUITAR HOCKEY

I LIKE WHEN AFTER A hockey player scores a goal and he bends down low to the ice, drags one knee on the ice, and makes a motion similar to playing a guitar. This brings to mind a new form of hockey, "Guitar Hockey!" Gary Glitter's Rock and roll part II at one time was the music that was played the most in ice rinks all around; perhaps it's time for Rock and Roll part III performed by the ice hockey team.

You can shoot, score, and play on the hockey-stick guitar your favorite victory song. Ahhh, the sounds of the sweet music of your success! As you receive the pass from your team mate before you break out of the neutral zone and skate into your opponent's end of the ice. Just before you wind up and shoot the puck towards the defending goalie; your teammates break out in unison with a selected song for the advance and attack. Just as the days of old when the bag pipers sounded off as the warriors marched into battle; you shoot and score to the sounds of the modern day guitar.

Another advantage is the hockey team can now be the warm-up band prior to the main band you wanted to see in concert using the hockey rink after the game. It doesn't get any better than that. Hockey and a concert all in the same evening! This guitar hockey drawing has me thinking about a similar sporting event for a future drawing . . . course at this time, music will not be a factor on the playing field as in Guitar Hockey . . . You'll see.

Before I began to ink in this drawing I noticed some things I wasn't pleased about. I planed to have a drawing for game three of the Stanley cup finals between the Boston Bruins and the Vancouver Canucks. Then Boston started scoring goals so I figured, "Why fix something that is not broken." There's one item in particular that is very noticeable and jumps out at you. I drew the logo on the Vancouver goalie shirt backwards. Maybe you didn't notice it as I suspected you would? Couple other things I didn't like were the drawing of the net and the position of the goalies legs in relation to his body . . . However, as I was saying the Bruins started scoring so, I wasn't going to change anything other than ink in over my pencil drawing. So I singularly caused the Boston Bruins to win the Stanley Cup Trophy, believe it or not. That's what I'm telling myself and I'm not changing my story. Yep, I did it! It had nothing to do with the skill and abilities of the professional hockey players themselves! Yep, me!

Are you a hockey fan? Would you be a fan of interest if the two teams played a hockey guitar? During the opening when the National Anthem or Anthems; if one team is from Canada and the other is from the United Sates both Anthems are played out of respect for the two countries. With the hockey teams strumming and jamming to the Anthems, this would only add to the sound of patriotism. I'm sure we can come up with some other sports that a musical instrument could successfully be applied too. Music calms the sole and refreshes the energy.

Quite a bonus when a musical performance is added to your sports game. Usually, the music that is played at sports events has to stop once play is resumed . . . No more will the music be required to stop! The music can play on, all through the game, and the fans can sing right along. Home advantage never sounded so good.

After watching a few games on TV, with friends and family that know the rules, the game becomes clear and understandable. For instance, the term icing has nothing to do with a player turning sideways, stopping quickly, and spraying ice in the air towards another player . . . It's when you're in your end of the arena defending your net and your clear the puck all the way to the other end of the rink and the other team touches the puck first. This is called Icing. A face-off will follow back where the icing originated from . . .

Attending a hockey game at the arena is wild. Very high energy from the fans and if you bring your children along, they may pick up a few words not taught in school! See that . . . hockey is educational.

You may have guess or figured out that I am a bruins fan, I watched my first games back in the days of Bobby Orr number four, Phil Esposito, Derek Sanderson, Pie face Mackenzie, just to name a few players. Oh yea . . . I do route for the local teams now that I live in California, however it's hard not to route for the teams from my youth. I'll always route for the Boston Red Sox and the Boston Bruins.

Baseball could use some sound amplifying devices that relay sounds to the PA system which would assist the umpire in making the correct call. They'd be planted in the gloves, bat, shoes, and ball. The gloves could amplify the sound of the ball contacting the glove. The balls could have a whizzing sound when thrown and a different sound once it makes contact with the bat. The bat and ball sounds could differ depending on whether it's a fowl, bunt, a solid hit or a homerun. Shoe sounds will be different depending on whether the batter is lumbering up to the plate (like a Yogi Bear walk.) What would be a good sound for a walk to first, stealing a base, or high tailing around the bases after a hit?

Outta Sbzzz Mind   by Sb Waitt

SbWaitt

Guitar Hockey

FIELD STRIPPING OF A SMALL ARM

IN THE ARMY, MARINES, NAVY and special weapons unit shows at the movies or on TV; the men or women using a fire arm, has to know to use the weapon inside and out. They can assemble and disassemble their weapon blindfolded. This degree of 'knowing your weapon,' was not something I had to do in my years of the navy; even though, I did at times carry a .45 CAL. Pistol or other weapons depending on the watch I was standing or the particular incident that arose.

So the term, "field stripping of a small arm," has me thinking about anything and everything that doesn't have to do with guns. The word small arms, for a person like me that didn't use guns prior to the navy or after my years served, has me imagining short stubby arms being ripped apart with a knife in a field.

The first time I fired a real riffle was in Boot camp at Great lakes Illinois. Yep, a real 22 riffle . . . "O boy," we were allowed to shoot 10 rounds. I believe we had about 1 hour of instruction and information and the actual shooting/firing was over in about 90 seconds. The words bellowed out loud and strong from the gunners mate in charge, "Ready on the right, ready on the left, ready on the firing line!" That was over 36 years or so ago, wow! How time flies.

Prior to the navy, I used to play army with the kids in the neighborhood. We'd use cap pistols, squirt guns, sticks, pieces of wood, and sometimes we had these nifty plastic rifles that made interesting sounds. Yes, that excited us in that particular period of our childhood. We might even have had a few helmets and utility belts between to add to the fake realism.

After boot camp aboard my various ships; I had training on other weapons such as the .45 CAL. pistol, shot gun, M14 riffle, .50 cal machine gun, and a 25mm canon, none of which I had to know how to strip down to parade rest. My favorite during the navy was the .50 CAL. on my third ship USS Leahy CG-17; I was part of the ship's close in attack team. Incase of a close in threat or attack, a bunch of us were trained to respond and man up the port and starboard .50 cal mounts just under the bridge wings.

One night in the Mediterranean Sea somewhere off the coast of Lebanon (gives or takes), while most of the crew was in there rack sleeping; at an about time of "Oh Dark thirty" the words sounded over the 1-MC(Main speaker information circuit for the ship) to man up the .50 cal mounts. I remember Bucky B and I, picked up our flax jackets, helmets and a couple cases of ammo cases, before we ran up on deck to our station (the port side gun mount.) Once on deck, we loaded the ammo into the ready position, I put on the sound powered phones and reported in, "Port side .50 CAL. mount manned and ready." We received information that an inbound unknown was at approximately 10 miles away and closing. We went recited to each other, what to do . . . over and over, in-between updates on the contact's information from the bridge? And then, we received the word, "Standby for command fire at will." That's when we discovered our gun wasn't chambering the rounds . . . You see when the official gunner's mates perform daily maintenance of the outside gun mounts and they can be set up for right or left feed. Me, being a sonarman, did not know that . . . "Huh, what could be wrong I," thought? We called up and reported in about the gun on the mount was not functioning correctly. Quickly a gunner's mate was sent to our station to rectify the matter. Shortly before the gunners mate arrived to our station the order was given to, "stand-down and remain on station!" The unknown in-bound became a known in-bound, it was a friendly know . . . After that incident it became a requirement for all gun mount teams to perform the required maintenance to the gun mount they were responding too, with the supervision of a knowledgeable and qualified gunners mate. Yea, my heart raced a little that night. It's a good and fun memory seeing as nothing tragic happened.

Since retiring from the navy I've never touched a real weapon, gun, firearm, or what ever you want to call them. I only did it in the navy because, that's what was required of me to do. Now I pass on the opportunity. Some times at a video arcade or on a computer I may do some shoot-em up blow-em up stuff and that's the closest I come to fire arms these days.

Field stripping of a small arm.

CONTOUR DRAWING NUMBER II

AS I MENTIONED IN AN earlier drawing, I'm very not fond of the drawing style called the Contour Drawing Technique. It is fun to draw about this dreaded drawing style; at least it's dreaded to me. No, I've thought about this for a while and I'm sure there are others that loathe this drawing style.

Have you ever attempted to draw a picture with your eyes closed? The outcome is interesting and is an art form in itself. I don't know if there is a technical name for it; drawing with your eyes closed that is. Perhaps, Linda, Fred, Meri, or Joe would be a good name? If you type in, "drawing with eyes closed" for a search on your computer you will find artist that have participated in drawing this way. I'd say it's an abstract form of art that reaches out from the inner soul.

Maybe this style with the eyes closed with a water color wash over, with your eyes closed, might be interesting. Possibly, after drawing with the eyes closed you might color in the squiggle lines with your eyes opened. One eye opened and one eye shut does not excite me. No offense intended to those artist with one eye. The possibilities are endless if you do tap into your inner soul.

The man that, made the wish to have the upper hand in life, now is suited for this drawing style called contour drawing. He can keep one set of eyes trained on the subject at all times, while the other head is trained on the canvas, paper, or what ever art medium you prefer. After all, four eyes are better than two.

From time to time he likes to draw using his teeth, which isn't too difficult seeing as he has two heads. After a few times drawing with his mouth and Idea came to him. He sent out a patent for flavored paint brushes, pens, and pencils. He doesn't mind the flavor of crayon as long as the paper is removed. He detests the flavor of chalk, "Yuck-o!"

If a couple of these guys got together, I wonder what would a hand wrestling event would be like? No biting below the waist! Hmmmm, how about attending an eating contest? Wouldn't it be interesting to watch, if he was one of the hungry participates.

If he never found that magic lamp he may never have found out that he is an artist. It's funny how an undesired event in time could turn out to be a good happening. At the time after the Gen fulfilled his wish he was very upset. The male genie of the lamp would not take back his wish? No the outcome between the Gen and the past archeologist that hasn't been determined, remember? So the Upper-hand man turned to art. He may now be known as the Contour Man. He enjoys the simple things in life even though he is twice smarter than anyone in existence today.

He may take up an invite from time to time and join in on an archaeology expedition; however, today his passion is drawing and painting. He'd like to figure out how he could take up sculpting. He's thinking outside of the box of what common people call normality. I'm sure he'll find a way; after all he is very intelligent. What he lacks in manual dexterity he makes up for with smarts. Yep, two heads are better than one.

He's planning on meeting up with the artist with the Seeing Eye dog. Together they will collaborate in something wild, new, and refreshing. When they do team up together they will be an unstoppable force. You could even say they are High Heel Rollers, course that's a nuttah drawing.

I still wonder if the contour man can be left brained in one head and right brained in the other head regardless of which head is on which side. Will this mean they are not dominate with one head and are ambidextrous? This is way too much to think about seeing as I only have one head and one brain. I'll be questioning this guy for a long time. Of course there are some people that aren't convinced I have a brain, they'll say, "prove it!"

Outta Sbzzz Mind   by Sb Waitt

Contour Drawing Number II

MEANWHILE IN THE LAND OF DROIDS

ON BOARD SHIPS THERE IS a device that is designed to shoot down in coming missiles called the Close in Weapons system (CWIS,) it's also known as the phalanx. The system resembles R2D2 from the Star Wars movies. I imagined in the land of droids that there is a compatible system which resembled a human being. I did design the human figure for the droid CWIS system after a fellow shipmate which I will not name. He's the mini radar and tracking system for the protection from inbound enemy air threats.

There is a newer gun system coming out that is better than the CWIS; however, that is up to someone else to draw. I've got zero knowledge about it. I've seen a few pictures . . . It doesn't look as cool as the R2 like devices. I may draw a system that emulates the robot from Lost in Space now that would be cool to me.

Drawing at sea, during the off time was fun and a bit challenging at times. A moving ship seldom travels level and smooth. It usually plows through the waves and bounces up and down at times due to the sea state from the wind. The ship will rock from side to side seldom siting still is a rarity. Drawing straight lines evenly spaced or any line that you desire becomes a slow and interesting encounter.

I'd get a kick out some of the comments and questions from my shipmates when I draw: "hey, you're pretty good." "How do you do that with all the bobbing we do in the water?" "Do you ever think about becoming an artist?" The last comment has always sent me off into space, dreamland, or someplace in my past. Do I ever think about being and artist, hmmmm. When does a person finally achieve the official title as, artist?

My favorite reaction from people is when they say," Ohhh, your and artist!" Now my experience from this comment is. When I'm being called and artist, what that person is really saying is, they want me to make them a sign. I don't know why, it just is! Making signs is my least favorite forms of art too me. Sign makers are artist and I'm glad that someone likes to make signs because I don't. I have created signs for several people over the years. When I do, I'm reminded that I don't enjoy it very well. In my early days as a draftsman, lettering is a requirement for each drawing. That was back before computers and auto-cad. I have taken classes in Auto-cad and it is faster and neater than the old hand and pencil method. No more eraser filings to brush off of your clothes or graphite smears on a white shirt.

What if caveman lived in a world where all life didn't have eyes to see by? Would he have discovered that fire was useful or would he have determined it was too dangerous? Being near fire, while blind, to me . . . must be frightening? How slow would it have taken for the technology of today to have developed? Would there have been a dark age and if so, what would it have been called? What kind of art would there have been? Perhaps a device to simulate sight might eventually be designed and built; art might not have happened until then? Maybe the art they created, we wouldn't have understood to be art?

Those things which we see and use may have not be designed the way are they are today if we humans were different in appearance. What if we had four arms instead of two, smelt color, or had some other type of sense to replace hearing. What would cars be like if we had four legs? Ice skating might be interesting? Dancing would be a trip, literally! What if hair was part of vision? What if your proboscis was only for balance?

On a silicon based world, where the air contains no oxygen or corrosive gases, could there have been lighting which sparked life into existence and this life have been in the form of a chip. No, not a potato or corn chip, something much like a computer chip, and somehow a ceramic-electrical or crystal-electrical life form evolved from this chip. Now somehow the lightening striking the elements around the chip in combination with the precipitation from the sky creates a power source which attaches itself to the chip. Maybe, sort of like crystals some fibrous strains grow and they attach them-selves to this power source and link other chips and composite like materials together to form an intelligent system.

This process may have started over and over and failed until one day the system stayed healthy enough to not loose it's power and produced electrical fields, magnetism, and other ways of transferring its energy to find and produce what it needed to create, build, and eventual reproduce and evolve. Yea, I don't know what I'm talking about; however, that's how wonderful new ideas are formed and developed. There might be a world where non-animal life formed and developed. Perhaps they branch out until they figure out how to leave their planet. (Don't be afraid to write down ideas no matter how strange they sound to you . . .)

Beware SETI and NASA when contact is finally made it may not be what you think. Biological life is one form of life only . . . what other unimaginable forms of life are out there transmuting around a not so distant star. There may be more than one way for an R2 unit to form?

OuttaSbzzzMind by SbWaitt

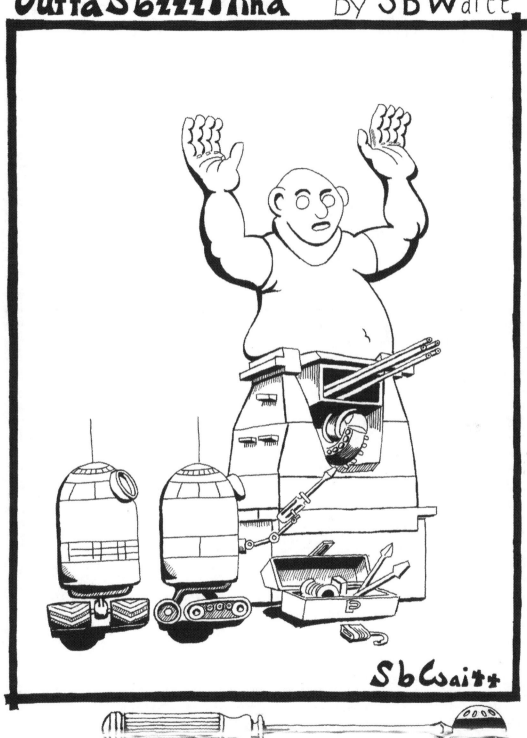

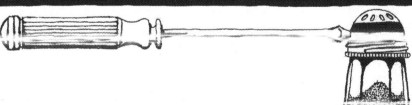

Meanwhile in the land of Droids.

"YOU WOULDN'T KNOW WHERE
YOUR HEAD WAS IF IT WASN'T ATTACHED!"

HOW MANY TIMES HAVE I heard this in my life time? I've been told, If ya hear something once about yourself that ya don't like you may go, "ahhh." Hear the same something twice it's, time to go, "Hmmmmm?" Now, hear the same comment about self a third time and it's time to start looking deep into self to see what is it about me that is giving this impression to other people, It's no longer a coincidence. I'm the common denominator in each case of receiving a comment about me that I don't like or ever believed. Clear as mud?

Listen and keep track of the various comments you receive from people. Good or bad write them down. Place a tick mark by them every time you receive a correlating comment. After the third time of hearing, for example, "You wouldn't know where your head was if it wasn't attached!" Start to reflect about the comment and not get up tight. Maybe ask some of the commenting people, "Could you please tell me what you mean by that?" With an open mind and your hands in your pockets unclenched, you will/may/might benefit from it.

Usually, when I heard this I'm a little distracted and not present with what is going on at the time. Yes, I didn't or don't always pay attention. Sometimes in class I would start doodling due to my lack of interest of the classroom subject matter and before you know it, I'm being called on by the teacher or instructor to answer a question that I have no idea or clue about; because, I shut the class off out ten minutes ago and my doodle is becoming more and more detailed. As time has gone on without any reason to pay attention I've gone totally into a fantasy and the picture has become real.

As I mentioned earlier in this book; where you paying attention and remember me talking about what I'm going to say? Are you not a mind reader? Ok, this is what I said before, "in grade school if the subject matter wasn't art, recess, lunch or going home I wasn't interested." This disinterest carried over to other aspects of my life such as: homework, mowing the lawn, taking out the garbage and rubbish barrels, making my bed, washing dishes . . . Come to think about it at home if it wasn't about me, having fun, watching TV, or eating . . . I wasn't too interested. One exception, teasing my youngest-older sister was a priority to me. Many a time she'd be starting her bath and I'd bang on the door and shout, "I have to go to the bathroom!" She'd come out in her bathrobe, I'd run in, turn on the cold water and shut off the hot and/or throw a hand full of the gummy like creepy-crawlers in the bath tub. Few minutes later I'd receive the satisfaction of hearing my name screamed out loud! I am very thankful she was never mean to me. It was that I was terrible to her! As I age in life and reflect about my home life growing up I find I dislike more and more about me.

My "first," fourth grade teacher, is the one person I remember sarcastically articulating to me on more than one occasion, this cliché about the head being attached; with the added bonus of facial expressions and varying tonal qualities. She was a tough teacher. In reality, as I look back, she was probably the kind of teacher that would have been better for my academic behavior right from the start of elementary school. That's all behind me now, physically! Mentally, I have a few vivid memories that I'd like to forget. Let's say teachers didn't have to be so politically correct back in those days. Near the end of that particular school year I really didn't care about school work to much. I even refused to make art project that she requested I do for the classroom bulletin board . . . I still remember the words, "If you don't do the bulletin board it will reflect on your art grade!" I responded, "I don't care."

Yes, I was now starting my fifth year of elementary school with my second, fourth grade teacher. She was nicer in my mind. I did work harder in her class and learned that a "C" was the lowest grade I ever want to receive on my report card. I figured it would be a lot easier the second time around, however, there were some changes like, new books! Why did we have to receive new books? I remember one of the books was in one on my least favorite of my least favorite subjects, "Geography?" Back then, I did like the pictures of the penguins of Antarctica. The Antarctican chapter was the shortest chapter and my favorite chapter in the book. Do you know how many penguins, in the wild, are eaten by polar bears every year? Come on, take a guess.

So today if I lose my head for real I want to be able and come back to do some haunting . . . Headless people figures are real good at scaring people. Maybe I'll make it on paranormal TV show. If'n Elvira is still around after I die. I'd like to team up with her from time to time and definitely make an appearance when she closes with, "Unpleasant dreams." Maybe, I'll follow her home . . . Hey, I'm dead.

Outta Sbzzz Mind by Sb Waitt

You wouldn't know where your head was if it wasn't attached!

SANTA JAWS

TODAY, I THOUGHT THIS WOULD make a good T shirt for the holidays, and if you have the holiday spirit all year round; please, feel free to wear it all year round! It would go good on a mug and card as well. This idea originated years ago, during the time frame mentioned in the next paragraph, just after my wife died in January of 1990. Since then, I've redrawn it a few times and this is how it's drawn today.

This was one of my dark pictures I drew when I was in the Arabian Gulf aboard USS Leahy CG-16 during the 1991/92 timeframe. I do have more; maybe, in the next book I'll share a few? I was asked to create some possible Christmas drawings, by the XO (executive officer, second in command) of my ship. The drawings were going to be placed in a family gram to our loved ones stateside, while we were operating overseas. A family gram is a newsletter about our deployment activities, which includes: port calls, work at sea, sailors being transferred to and from our ship, how much we miss and can't wait to see you again stuff. I presented a bunch of my creations to my Executive Officer; he thought that my sketches and drawings were a little bizarre and morbid for Christmas. He said, "Chief, what's this? I'm not going to use any of these drawings in a letter to the families! These aren't in the spirit of Christmas!" I wasn't feeling the spirit at that time I was still grieving. He paused, looked at the picture some more, shook his head, and then he looks at me in the eyes and said, "Chief, draw me a picture of Santa in his sleigh being pulled by camels." I did draw what he asked for and it did go into the family newsletter.

Come to think about the morbid drawings. I drew some doodles even before my wife's death that were on the morbid side. I was very sarcastic about safety helmets and shoes during the ship yard period of my stay on the Leahy. I believe during the grieving process I slid a little deeper down the dark path. Now I view my darkness as an expression to draw and share. I find most people have dark thoughts and they are afraid to tell and admit anything about them. If, I may be so bold . . . some people lie about their dark inner thoughts and the dreams at night. To admit to a dark thought will destroy ones façade. Hey, why is there a little thingy attached to the letter 'c' in the word façade?

I wonder if sharks have the holiday spirit. Every time they catch a fish to eat it must feel like a present to them. When their bellies are full, they can continue to swim and exist for another day, and the process continues. The fish don't feel any spirit. They only feel the teeth chomping down on their body. Imagine being chewed to death. Big ouch and the last pain you will ever experience!

In horror movies we see zombies snacking on people's arms, legs and inner parts. I've had a few nightmares over the years about being chased by creatures. I turn my head these days on a lot of violence I use to intentionally go to the movies to watch. How about getting mauled by a tiger; my imagination and mind becomes enmeshed with movies and it's as if I am in the movie for real living and dying as the actor's perform. There is a song "Tiger" by Abba . . . "I am behind you, what if I find you, what if I eat you, I am the Tiger." I wanted to be mauled by Abba in my youth . . . I was watching the "Alien" movie last week . . . It still scares me. Can you imagine having a creature bit, eat, and claw its way out of your stomach?

If I watch the shark movies today and I squirm . . . These are movies, I didn't budge, flinch, or turn my head away from and I'd sometime laugh at. years ago. I don't laugh much anymore at these movies; they were never intended to be laughed at unless they are real cheesy movies, you know below the 'B' movie category. As I age I have a different outlook in life and don't relish the thought of dying in gross pain.

My friends say, "Sb, you draw some terrible stuff yet you're afraid of heights, needles, and gross stuff on shows and movies . . . You cry when people and animals are hurt and die! Yet you can write and draw about all that stuff, why is that?" Drawing and writing is different. Again I say to you, movies have a way of luring me into the screen and I'm no longer watching the movie . . . I am living it all out as if I am there for real! After a while I don't notice the boarder around the movie screen, see the people in front of me, or dip into the popcorn; enmeshment to the max!

With my charity group I have dressed up as Santa Claus several times over the years past 10 years. It is a very memorable and rewarding experience. Lots of hugs and smiles, oows and aaahs, and if I throw in a few, "ho ho ho's," the children's eyes light up big, wide, and bright. The holiday season doesn't come fast enough; although, the years seem to fly by faster and faster. I like having someone with me to run interference. When I play Santa I don't like to traumatize little children or babies. So if the children are crying, attempting to run away from moms and dads who are shoving and dragging the children as they scream, kick, and yell their lungs out. My helper says politely, "Your child isn't ready at this time for Santa; perhaps, she/he will warm up to the experience as they watch others walk up to Santa." Sometimes children enjoy Santa from a distance yet not close up. I think, they're envisioning me as 'Santa Jaws!'

Outta Sbzzz Mind   by Sb Waitt

Santa Jaws

"I'VE GOT VOICES IN MY HEAD, MAKE 'EM STOP!"

DO YOU HEAR THE VOICE or voices talking in your head? I'm sure you do whether you admit it or not. That's the committee in your head. It's always jabbering away when you're talking or not talking, reading, listening, being chewed out, being lectured, or have doubt about what your doing comes to mind. The voices seem to be there in the mind constantly. If you don't believe me sit down for two minutes and attempt to turn off all the noise. The voices will be singing, talking, and screaming at you to knock-off the silent treatment. Ever go to a lecture and sit quietly . . . those voices may say something to the effect of, "When is she/he gonna stop talking, I've heard all this before, maybe they'll fall down, why does she/he keep fiddling with the glasses and clicking the pen, I wonder if my show is recording, Did I turn off the stove this morning, blaaa bla blaaa . . ." it'll go on and on as long as you sit there in your set. Even when talking to your friends your mind dances all over the place.

I think my voices come from my inner children. There was a time when people talked about the inner child I would smirk, laugh and think, "Boy are they crazy, inner child, hawwww!" So I've come from not believing that I have an inner child all the way to finding and believing that I have inner children.

If your wondering, I do not have clothes in my closet that I'm not sure who they belong too or have things that I'm not suppose to touché in my own home even though I live alone. I'm at a point in my life that I believe wherever I have had trauma (To what ever degree) a piece of me stopped growing and hid somewhere inside.

So perhaps you think "I'm" crazy? Well, I think that's funny, now! One of my heroes from my past (Red Skelton) was and still is. He said something to the affect, "you may think I'm nuts . . . and I probably am, however, as long as I keep them laughing they're not going to lock me up!" So as long as people like my drawings, art work, and/or stories . . .

Trauma can be in many forms such as; physical, psychological, emotional, and there is probably more . . . And the more I hear about body memory; I believe there is trauma there as well. It's like the first time you didn't believe what a friend told you so you weren't going to do what he wanted and you got hit, slapped or they refused to be your friend anymore. So a part of you now does not like confrontation with people. Possibly, when you are in a position of confrontation (like me) you go into your child like route. Adult as a possibility does not exist and you act childish. When I let my emotions take over for the most part I'm in one of my childlike routes, yell back, sarcasm, run away and hide, ramp up and rage, talk a lot of nonsense, or meltdown on the spot. "When," I think a little . . . I step back and feel my emotions going wild and realize what is going on . . . That is when I don't react. Personal growth seminars and other types of group meetings are helpful to me which helps me to allow my inner children grow.

Sometime though, the voices come from the subliminal side or my creative being. Expression on paper for me is a good thing. I have a tangible picture in front of me to help me reflect. What ever I just said? It's a good thing to express in words, writing, drawing, music, activities, etc . . .

What I don't care for is when the committee in my head slams doors, drags the chairs around the room, plays music very loud, scrapes the chalkboard with there fingernails or shouts . . . you know, stuff like that is annoying and distracting and can be very rude. Specially, at movie theaters when the person sitting next to me hears the committee in my head. They may tap me on the shoulder and say, "excuse me. Please be quiet I'm listening to a movie here!"

Does anyone use chalkboards anymore? Listening to the sound of fingernails scratching a chalkboard will make your skin crawl! Well, at least it does for me. All someone has to do is make a motion to scratch a chalkboard with their fingers and I turn inside.

Of course the voices could me coming from the vortex or you have little people running around your house. Yes it could be the results of an alien abduction from last night or years ago. Maybe the aliens placed an implant in your brain. At any given minute, the creatures listening and watching you can flip a switch so they can transmit voices and images directly into your mind. No escape and running will do you any good . . . You've be tagged for life or until the device becomes defective and that could be worse. Would you rather have voices that you can distinguish or broke words and sentences, squeaking sounds, tonal hums, perhaps the devise now picks up TV and radio signals . . . Yep it's gonna be crazy, noisy. and uncomfortable for ya . . . It won't be long before you check into an insane asylum.

Outta Sbzzz Mind by Sb Waitt

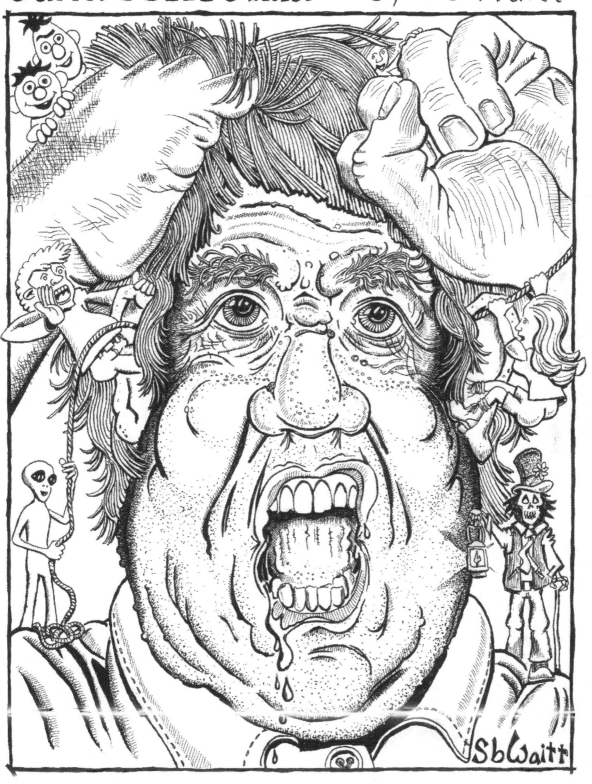

"I've got voices in my head, make 'em stop!"

BIG ANIMALS FOR LITTLE KIDS

Biganimalsforlittlekids.com

BIG ANIMALS FOR LITTLE KIDS is an organization that entertains special needs children. Please check out our website at biganimalsforlittlekids.com and we are on Facebook as well . . . We do lots and lots good stuff. We'd love for you to stop by and check us out sometime and if you like, keep coming back and tell your friends us about Big Animals for Little Kids and have your friends tell their friends so those friends to tell their friends, and on and on and on . . . We are always looking for good helpers and good people to become involved. We'd love for you and them to become us as in one big family . . . We do lots of fun things with each other besides the charity work so there is always a friendship relation or possibility to develop as well.

So, you may ask, "How did I become involved with this organization", well . . . It was in the year of 2000 around late spring, early summer time and I was attending one of the Friendship Parties I enjoyed. Friendship Parties was and is a fun get together for eating, dancing, a fashion show, and a lot of mixing and meeting: as part of a personal growth seminar that I've been involved with since 1995 . . . Like I was saying I was at this party and I was waiting to talk with a friend. My friend Steve (who I meet in a seminar) was talking to someone else (Frank, which I did not know at the time) and I didn't want to cut in; so, I stood there and listened to the two of them talk about dressing up in animal costumes and entertaining children. Finally, they stopped talking and then I talked with Steve. He shared with me what he had talked with Frank about and said there was going to be a cookout at his house and there would be a sign-up sheet for all interested. So weeks later I attended the cookout at Frank's house on the beach . . . There was also another event going (more fun seminar parties) on at his house at the same time so there was a lot of food, singing, mixing and mingling, and dancing going on. After some music the DJ introduced Frank and he gave a speech about his idea for a great charity group . . . He gave a little history about how it all started with all the 'who, what, when, where, how, and why stuff.' He then said, "There is a sign-up sheet for those interested in making this charity come into existence, formally." There was a date, time, and location where we would all meet for the first time.

We meet at Frank's house for the first organized meeting and we began to meet weekly after that continually at Frank's house to organize, make phone calls to various groups and organizations asking if they would like our service to add to their events, and we'd continue to call friends to come join us or ask if they knew anybody that might be interested. We were alive and kicking and soon we became an official not for profit organization; I forget which meeting we agreed on the name of Big Animals for Little Kids.

I remember sometimes when funds were low, we'd pull money out of our pockets and wallets, throw our money on the table, and do whatever was necessary to make events work for the children. We didn't have a stockpile of stuff for future events in the beginning. We'd buy and pick up the supplies, and rent costumes the day before an event.

As we slowly grew we would receive donations for costumes and we'd buy second hand costumes. Soon we didn't have to rent as much. Lorraine joined us and she hand made some of our earlier costumes. Eventual someone had the Polaroid's, someone else had the film, this person had the balloons and pumps, someone else had the face paints, and etc . . . our supplies were scattered at different people's houses. This scattering of supplies made it difficult to maintain an inventory, so I volunteered my three car garage around the beginning of the 2001 time frame. What started out to be a few costumes, and various supplies that took up a very small area of my garage ended up, over the years, taking over about ¾ of my garage. We even got involved with toy drives for the holiday season in December, so my house inside was now loading up with toys as well. Before I realized it my home became headquarters. I don't remember how many in the group had keys to my house. I wanted the house to be open and available at all times, regardless of me being home or not.

Around 2008 we became a 501.3(c) organization. We now participate in 40-50 events a year. This past January/February of 2011 the group moved out of my home and into a warehouse. It' feels funny not having my garage and home over run with animal supplies. Lost count how many times I'd come home to a house full of people and the sound of the washing machine running (sweaty costumes must be washed or they'll mildew.) There usually was something going on at my house a few days or so out of the month besides prepping for the next event and dropping of stuff from the events; like: costume parties for repair and service, face painting parties, planning parties, holiday box wrapping parties, and other parties . . . I was never lonely specially since as we perform about 40 events a year plus monthly meetings . . .

Outta Sbzzz Mind   by Sb Waitt

Big Animals for Little Kids

Well there ya have it, you're almost at the end of my book. I told ya there might be a short test at the end. "Test first and teach later," my fortune cookie always said. So you ask, "Why isn't this test at the beginning of the book?" My reply, "Ahhh, it doesn't fit into a fortune cookie?" Yes I know a small chip can fit inside a fortune cookie. Well, you do that when you write your book.

THE TEST SORT OF

1. What is your name?
2. What is your favorite TV show?
3. Where is the birth place of the US Navy? See below *** (special note)
4. What is the best thing you like about yourself?
5. What comes to mind after looking and reading this book?
6. What is the name of my dentist?
7. What was my profession before joining the navy?
8. Does spell check work when you write in wing ding?

Essay/English/language portion

1. Write a 25,000 word essay on how you are going to change the world. Ok, if you can write it in 25 words or less. Cause you're going to change the world in some way. I believe in you! I know you'll add to this essay over the years with more detail.
2. Correct my gramma and tell the publisher.
3. When people ask me what does, "Je ne Sais pas" mean? I always reply, "I don't know?"

Math questions

1. State the Pythagorean Theorem. _Clue_ _it's more than just A squared plus B squared equals C squared._ You know a verbal explanation without a diagram.
2. In third angle projection a straight line perpendicular to a plane of projection will show as what in the adjacent views?
3. If you add up all the questions together in the math portion, what would your answer be? _Two, Three, Six, Not enough information, I wasn't paying attention, may I be excused? I have to go to the bathroom!_

History and Religion

1. None . . . Noah built and sailed the ark, gathered the animals onto the ark as they came to him . . . Not Moses
2. So if a girl or woman writes a history book will it be called a Herstoty Book?

Geography

1. So, did ya figure out how many penguins are eaten in the wild by polar bear

*** Note: My Gramma was a wonderful cook! End of note.
*** Another note: I never talked about my dentist so you don't know.
*** A third note: Really it's a question, is a 1/3 note faster than a full note?
*** Last note for now: again a question, did you take notes . . . if they're mine, put em' back please. Oh yea, some answers you'll have to find out for yourself. That's life.
*** Note to the gramma police. I likes ta misspell words on poaypose specially cause I know it goes against the rules . . .
*** (special note) Warning my answer may cause an error, mistake, or your answer to be marked wrong on a real test in collage . . . The correct answer is Marblehead, for now! Beverly calls themselves the: Birthplace of Washington's Navy. However if your debating that opens up more possibilities!

IN CONCLUSION

SO WHAT IS/ARE YOUR INTEREST in life? How do you like to be creative? Do you like to draw, sing, doodle, paint, dance, write, play an instrument, tell stories, stain glass, decorate, candle maker, basket weaver? Do you hear those voices saying, "You're not good enough?" Perhaps you've experienced some difficult times so you put your creativeness away till "someday?"

Guilt held me back for years. While in my Junior High School, my dad gave me an option of taking organ lessons or art? I choose art. My dad had me send in one of those, "Draw Me" pictures. You know the ad that asks, "Do you like to draw?" I drew the picture and sent it in. A week or so later I receive another test. I completed the test and mailed it in. A few weeks later an agent was sent out to my house to talk with my parents and me. I was all excited. The first 6 lessons I worked on at home and then something hit me. It wasn't fun. I liked a class room environment. I hated mailing in questions and waiting for a reply. I got to the point where I sent it in right or wrong. I finally lost interest in the course and was dis-enrolled. For years I carried the guilt of, I failed, I'm no good, and I'm not worthy. I still drew on my own however the feelings inside always surfaced. When my Dad died I became even more guilty about not completing the at home course.

I did enroll from time to time in an art course at a night school. I believe the turning point was when a soon to be friend of mine named Frank (this is a different Frank from the one mentioned about the charity group) suggested reading the book, Artist Way by Julia Cameron. I bought the book and there it sat on the shelf with a bunch of other, "shelf-help books." No, that's not a misprint or spelling error. I said, "shelf-help books," I call them shelf-help books because that's where they sit, unread, and on the self.

About a year later I heard a friend was offering an evening course designed around this book. I enrolled, dusted off the book, and participated. For the next 12 weeks I read the chapter of the week, did the assignments, and came to class for the next chapter. What I liked about the class is it wasn't just an information class. We also played and thought outside of the box. Sometimes, while reading about the chapter of the week in the class, we'd use crayons and glitter, we cut out pictures from magazines and begin a collage, listen to music and write, and lots of other different things that would help us to open up with creativity. Another Thank you goes out to Kat for being the facilitator though the course 'Artist Way' and being in my life. I highly encourage anyone to take this course. Please don't let your definition of what an artist is to get in your way from participating in this course or from reading the book.

If you need a qualifier to see yourself as an artist, here ya go. Have you ever colored in a coloring book? Ever sang out loud to a song? Ever doodled on a napkin or piece of paper? Ever cooked? Ever thought about writing a book after a class assignment? Ever danced in private or publicly with friends? Ever participate in a school play? How about, painted a room, rearranged furniture, folded a paper airplane, ice/roller skated, sewn, arranged rocks in your yard, and the list goes on. These are forms of creativity and expression. Many daily tasks and choirs can be and are a form of art. The artist way can help us/we/them to think outside of the box so we see and believe about the creative person we are.

Creative parenting is an art form. We didn't come with instructions on how to be. We managed and became! At work we are creative about exciting, enthusing, motivating our workers so they accomplish the required tasks.

If you're religious, think about this: God Created man in his image . . . Creation is creating, creating is creativity, and creativity is art . . . We are a reflection and were born to create, hence . . . "We are artist."

May you have enjoyed the drawings and the writings? You now know a little bit about me or maybe you know more about me that you wanted too.

Printed in the United States
By Bookmasters